BEGINNING OVER

A CANDLEWOOD FALLS NOVEL

STACEY WILK

～

This book is dedicated to the amazing women of Evolve Pink. It is an honor and a privilege to know you.

PRAISE FOR STACEY WILK'S BOOKS

Through the Darkness "Wilk pens a heart gripping story that will leave you breathless." *Jen Talty, USA Today Bestselling Author*

The Essence of Whiskey and Tea: "If you enjoy a good series about family and love, then this novel is sure to soothe your soul." *Booktrib*

Time Won't Erase: "The power of redemption shines in this emotional story about second chances." *Caridad Pineiro, New York Times and USA Today Bestselling Author*

Taking Root: "…multiple layers of entertainment." *InD'Tale Magazine*

Whispering Christmas: "She makes you feel deeply for each character as if you a part of the Candlewood Falls family." *Mint Copy Services*

Defining Chances: The author masterfully weaves together real-life situations, creating a narrative that's both thought-provoking and emotionally resonant. You'll find yourself rooting for Ember and Raf as they navigate their troubled pasts and learn to let go of guilt and anger. *Hidden Gems Reviews*

HAVE WE GOT A STORY FOR YOU!

Dear Readers:

Welcome to Candlewood Falls!

Each Candlewood Falls story stands alone. However, the end of one story doesn't mean the end of your favorite characters. They can show up in any Candlewood Falls book at any time.

Candlewood Falls is a unique world of connected stories by different authors whose characters, business, and events appear in each others' stories.

Think of Candlewood Falls as a literary soap opera.

Be sure to check out the Ready for Another Trip to Candlewood Falls page at the end to discover which other books include your favorite characters.

Happy reading!

Stacey Wilk, K.M Fawcett, & Jen Talty

CHAPTER ONE

No one said life was easy. But why was it hard?

Petra Wilde built another packing box. She folded flaps until they touched, not an overlap, but also no space that could be seen between the edges, and dragged the clear tape over the center. The packing tape left its roll in squealing protest. She kind of felt the same way. She objected to this project.

This box would make ten. She wasn't sure how many she would need. Probably more than ten, considering how many rooms she would have to strip. She ripped off another piece of tape to firmly secure the bottom before putting it aside. Better to have more than enough boxes ready to go because if she ever got up the nerve to pack her mother's belongings, she would need something to put the stuff in. Stuff. Junk. Valuables.

No matter what her father said, she wasn't ready to clear away every piece of evidence of her mother's life. She had promised to help, though. Had stepped up to assist her father in dealing with his grief. Wasn't that what a good daughter did? She tossed another box into the corner of the dining room. Eleven. The pile had climbed up the window like cardboard ivy, blocking the light.

"It's weird being here without Grandma and Grandpa." Her daughter, Paige, leaned against the doorframe. Her brown hair parted in the middle and slightly waved past her shoulders. Her blue-eyed gaze planted squarely on her phone while her thumb slid over the screen as she scrolled through some social media app.

Paige had a point. She couldn't remember a time when both her parents were not here. When her father returned in four weeks, he would return alone. The plan was to help his wife leave this world with dignity, and then he would take some time for himself. She hated that plan. But at least they had one.

In the meantime, she and Paige would live in the home Petra had grown up in with her two sisters, Ember and Nyx. Both of whom had wonderful lives. Her life was supposed to be wonderful too. She had done everything that was expected of her in order to keep the house of cards she had built. The cards had fallen. And the fruits of her hard labor had rotted clean through. So much for the best-laid plans. But she still craved a plan for herself the way she sometimes craved a Belgian waffle covered in strawberries.

"Why don't we get out for a while? We can stop by the community college and sign you up." She tossed the last box at the pile, knocking it all to the ground. There was irony.

"I'm not going to college." Paige's gaze snapped up. Her blue irises turned to storm-cloud gray. "How many times do I have to say it? College isn't for me."

"Then what do you plan on doing?" Paige had completed one year of higher education, but had come home in May to state with complete certainty that she refused to return. She hated the school, the kids, the classes, the food, and the smell. Petra hadn't bothered to inquire what the smells were exactly.

"I don't know."

"Just take a couple of classes while you figure things out." She really didn't know what *things* Paige needed to figure out. What nineteen-year-old had figured out anything? Hell, she was in her forties and still trying to figure things out. Taking a class or two wasn't going to hurt, and if anything it might help her narrow down a direction. Petra would like a direction that didn't include packing up this house.

"I'm not going. Stop trying to force me. You didn't want to go to college. And you resent Grandpa for making you go."

Nothing like having her own words thrown in her face. "That's not the way it went. I didn't want to major in business. Grandpa wouldn't pay for my education otherwise." And yes, she did resent her parents for not supporting her desire to go to culinary school. Someday, she would deal with that resentment, but it wouldn't be today.

"I'm not you, Mom. You made your decision. And I'm making mine. No college." Paige stormed out of the room. Her heavy footsteps pounded on the wooden staircase. The slam of a door punctuated the end of the scene.

"Well, you screwed that one up," she said under her breath. If she closed her eyes, she could transport back to the moment when a younger Paige would ask her to brush her hair or help with a ponytail Paige had lost control of. She could still smell the bubble gum-scented shampoo that Paige had loved so much. Now, her daughter had one foot out of the door, eager to take on the world and prove her mother wrong on every front.

Time was a tease. It paraded out every second the way a pole dancer left little to the imagination in the way of a costume. But like that pole dancer who could tantalize but not be touched, time wouldn't share one second more of itself for any price and would gladly run away without warning when no one was looking.

Her daughter was nearly twenty—okay, not quite yet but soon—and yet Petra didn't know where the time went. She had put in the hours, the late nights, and still the idea that Paige was an independent young lady mystified her. When did this happen?

Paige hadn't asked to come to Candlewood Falls. She hadn't wanted to move, but Paige's parents had successfully messed up her life. Petra would take the blame for that as well. Except she hadn't been alone.

Her ex-husband had his fist in the problem too. He had blown through their money without so much as a warning. She had allowed Frank to influence her every decision, saying it was what was best for their family. It had been what was best for Frank. And now they had nothing. No marriage, no house, no money. And worst of all, she had a daughter pissed as hell at her. But rightfully so. Expecting her parents to be a safe haven wasn't too much to ask.

Her phone rang. She dug through the clutter on the table and yanked it free just in time to swipe and answer.

"Hey, sis." She wedged the phone between her ear and shoulder and constructed another box.

"Hi. Would you and Paige like to come for dinner tonight? I want you to meet Raf. You're going to love him." Ember's cheery voice floated across the line. Ember had returned to Candlewood Falls four months ago and completely turned her life around. She met a man, moved in with him on day one, fell in love, and started a business. All without a plan. All without thought. But that was Ember. Her spontaneity usually worked out for the best—for her.

"Thanks, but I have some errands to run, then I want to come back, sit outside with a bottle of wine, and watch the fireflies." She was not up for socializing. She could spend time Raf later.

"You shouldn't drink alone. How about if we bring dinner to you? Let someone cook for you for a change."

"Cooking relaxes me. I just want some time alone tonight. How about you two come here tomorrow and I make dinner? I need to go to the grocery store because there is nothing in this house. I'll pick up something I can throw on the grill. Dad said the grill still works. And then I can meet your man Raf when I'm not so exhausted. I don't want him to think I'm the not fun sister."

Ember chuckled. "It's hard for any of us to compete with Nyx. She is some stiff competition."

"Yes, she is. So at least give me a head start. The house is hot, and I'm sweaty. I don't want to be smelly too." August in New Jersey didn't often provide a cool breeze, especially in Candlewood Falls which was surrounded by rolling hills. She had thrown open all the windows, but to no avail. She and the house were hotter than a deep fryer.

"Okay, okay. No dinner tonight. You do know the air conditioners are in the attic? Do you need help putting them in the windows? I can come over and do that with you."

"Paige and I can handle it. But thanks." She and Paige had only arrived a week ago. There hadn't been time to search the attic yet. Well, that wasn't an entire truth. She wasn't ready to face what lay in wait up in that attic. Unfortunately, they'd been sweating their backsides off because of her.

"And what about... you know... Mom's stuff? You shouldn't have to pack it all yourself. Let me help you with that at least."

"You have a brand-new business to run, and I'm sure Raf wants to have you around. I'm here to take care of the house." She needed to feel useful while she roamed around this house, even if she was dreading the task. The least she could do for her mother was organize the objects of her life.

"Raf is barely going to miss me. August through November is the orchard's busiest season. Dad always told us it was every season, but now I have a more realistic perspective. I won't be seeing much of Raf until Thanksgiving."

Ember's boyfriend worked the fields as the second-in-command under their cousin Brad who was the vice president of operations. Their father was also a vice president, but of distribution. Huck never liked being equal to his nephew and only tolerated Raf. It was a huge improvement from his original feelings for him. And strangely enough Huck had tried to change for Ember. Miracles never ceased.

"If I need any help, I'll let you know. I don't think I will though. What else am I going to do all day around here?"

"Are you really only going to stay until Dad comes back?"

"Ember, I have no idea what I'm going to do for dinner, never mind four weeks from now." She went into the kitchen and poured a glass of water from the tap. It was cool on her tongue and throat, but not cold enough. Never enough. Wasn't that her life summed up in a short sentence? She hadn't loved Frank the right way. She had never had a real career either.

"Wouldn't it be great to live in the same town again? We could do all kinds of things together."

"I need a job." Although, she didn't know what she wanted to be. She had taught preschool for many years, but quit four years ago to help Frank with his business. Preschool was okay, but she didn't want to return to the land of runny noses and stinky behinds.

"I needed a job too when I got here. I found one. You will too."

"I'm not like you. I can't start a business out of thin air and make it work. Besides, I don't just jump into things. Look how long it took me to leave Frank."

"Well, maybe you should have left sooner. But we all make mistakes. Look at me. I took Keith back twice before I figured out we weren't right for each other. And boy, am I glad I did. If I hadn't, I wouldn't have bumped into Raf. And now I can't imagine my life without him."

"I'm not going to just bump into my dream man in Candlewood Falls. That only happens to you and in romance novels."

"You're getting to be such a cynic in your old age. I have to run. I've got cookies ready to come out of the oven. Raf and I will see you and Paige tomorrow night around six. I'll bring the wine and the cookies."

"Thanks, Ember. I can't wait to see you."

"Me too. It's going to be okay, Petra. It always is. Love you." Ember ended the call.

Even though she had wanted her freedom, having it still tasted like foreign food to her. She never imagined she'd be back in her childhood home either. But here she was. She had better make the most of it. Somehow.

She would rather pull her eyebrows out than make another packing box. She would go to the college and register Paige. Once Paige was set, she would be more likely to go to school. And if Paige came up with a better idea, then fine. But at least she would have a plan. More than Petra had. All she had was a bunch of empty boxes and a hankering for some comfort food. After the school, she'd stop at the grocery store. Everything went better with homemade mac and cheese. Paige's favorite. It would soften the blow when she heard about school. Or maybe she'd make a summer salad with apple wedges and goat cheese. Her stomach was growling. Answers could always be found in food.

She jotted a quick text to Paige. *Running out. Be back soon. Want anything from the store?*

The reply came straight away. *NTY.*

Well, that was better than screw off. Petra smirked and grabbed her keys. At last she had a plan—albeit a small one. After she signed up her daughter for school, then she could figure herself out. But that would take a whole lot longer. And life, as she had said, was never easy.

CHAPTER TWO

He missed his garden. Maverick Labraccio juggled three brown paper bags of groceries—mostly veggies—up the cement stairs of his tired and sad apartment building to the second floor. The outdoor corridor was long with apartments on the right and a precarious metal railing on the left. The key to his door sat nestled deep in his shorts pocket, which would require him to put down the bags in order to retrieve it unless he dropped everything over the railing in the meantime.

The summer heat weighed him down, making every step seem like two. He wished for a cool breeze or a swim in a pool. He wasn't going to get either today. This sorry excuse for a residence, the home he hadn't planned on living in for so long, didn't have a pool. It did, however, have a lot of noisy kids playing in the courtyard area. Or maybe it should be called the court concrete area because other than a few weeds sticking through the cracks in the ground, nothing resembled a yard down there.

His abode also had a nosy neighbor who often perched

right outside her door with her hand firmly clutching closed the collar of her housedress, a pinch to her mouth that made his cheeks hurt. But Gladys was ninety and always nice to him.

His phone vibrated against his leg in the other shorts pocket. He wasn't expecting any calls, so whoever it was could wait. He had no choice but to place the bags down by the door. It shouldn't bother him so much, but the pettiest things did these days. He was starting to sound like his father. He blamed the sour moods on getting older, but he knew better.

The phone started up again. He shoved the key in the door and dug the phone free. A request for a video call— from Avery Hausman. His breath stuck in his throat. Why her? Why now? He tried to decline the call, but hit accept by accident. Or maybe he was just trying to torture himself.

"Mav, you picked up. I'm so glad." Half of Avery's round face and short blond hair filled the screen. She sat right on top of the camera, practically distorting her features like a fun house mirror. He and Avery had tried keeping in touch after his life was destroyed, but after a while there was very little to say without all the pain surfacing like an oil slick. Just being around her had made him want to drink back then. He had to stop speaking to her so he could stop drinking. After that, she'd call at the holidays to see if he was still breathing. He didn't understand why she cared. He had ruined her life too.

"Hi, Avery. What's up?" He quickly glanced at the screen, but didn't bother with the camera angle any more than she had. He needed to get his perishables out of the heat and into the fridge. If he still had a garden, he would have been able to pluck whatever vegetables he wanted right from his backyard. *But whose fault was that?*

"I need to ask a favor." She shifted the thin brown band holding her hair back. Her black glasses were too big for her face and made her eyes rounder, giving her a perpetual surprised look.

He put the phone down on the counter so he could move around the kitchen freely. They didn't need to see each other. Her voice was enough. "What's this favor?"

"Mav? Mav? Where did you go? I can only see the ceiling. Did I lose you?" Her voice was frantic as if they were in a crowded subway and she wasn't sitting squarely in front of her bookcase, looking at a screen.

To this day he was perplexed by the fact Avery was his late wife's sister. No two people could be more opposite. Avery was a violin string turned too tightly. And his wife... well, she had been the soft strum of an acoustic guitar at a twilight picnic. "I'm right here. I just need to be hands free. What's the favor, Avery?" He bit back the words to hurry her up, but he wasn't so sure his tone hadn't said everything he didn't.

"Well, if you remember, I took that job at the community college in Hunterdon County last spring."

He hadn't remembered. She may have mentioned it. He didn't always listen. "Sure."

"One of my teachers took a really bad fall and can't teach a class. It's not a full semester class, but one we're running for four weeks to see if there's a call for that kind of course."

"Avery, what kind of class and why are you telling me?"

Her sigh was as heavy as the afternoon heat. "Jeez,

Mav, let me get it out. I need a replacement teacher for the class. I'm hoping you'll do it."

"Do what? I can't teach. I work in a warehouse."

"It's a cooking class. I need a chef." Her words faded with each syllable as if she didn't want him to completely hear her.

He glanced at the screen, but his vision blurred with red. "I can't believe you of all people would have the nerve to ask me to teach a cooking class." He didn't cook for others any longer. Hadn't in years and her asking him to teach people to cook was just as insensitive. He had given up that life for a very good reason.

"It's been three years, and you're the best chef I know. Even still. I wouldn't ask if I wasn't in a bind. If this class doesn't go off, I could lose my job. I begged my boss to allow me to create a culinary arts program for the school. We need one to compete, but he doesn't think so. He says cooking isn't the wave of the future. No one wants to major in cooking. He thinks culinary arts is the same thing as home economics."

He squeezed his tomato hard enough to pop it, spraying the juice and the seeds all over his shirt and the counter. Cooking was an art form when done correctly. Everything from the food choices, the pairing of flavors, to the design on the plate was an expression of emotion. Home economics was an antiquated idea from the American high schools of the nineteen sixties that women should know how to sew. "Your boss sounds like a dumbass."

"He is, but he still has the power to fire me. Without a teacher, I'm screwed. Please, Mav. I need your help."

"Absolutely not. I'm sorry you wasted your time, but

my days in a professional kitchen are over. You know that and still you came to me with an impossible ask. You need to find someone else." Maybe he could check around quietly with some of his old colleagues and see if anyone was looking for a part-time gig. He hadn't kept in touch with really anyone from that time, but he could nudge a few stones.

"You really are the most stubborn person I have ever met. You're wasting away in that crappy apartment with that awful job you have. Don't even pretend that you don't mind. I knew you before. There's no way you want to get up every day and go to work. Come teach for me. You'll be the reason the program gets picked up."

He didn't appreciate being used. Avery was leveraging his past success. There was a time when he was the most sought-after chef on the East Coast. Him teaching would have been laughable once. "I've got to go. I appreciate you thinking of me, but it's a solid no." He hovered his finger over the end button.

"Shelby would have wanted you to help me," Avery said in a rush. Her face was still too close to the screen. The close-up gave him a good shot of her one red eye filling with tears.

The guilt tried to wag his tongue into agreement, but he clamped his lips down. Even if he wanted to, which he didn't, he couldn't cook anymore. Not like that anyway. His passion for food was gone. It had died that night too.

Avery must have taken his silence for waffling. "If you won't do it to help me save my job, then do it for her. Help your late wife's sister out of a jam. You owe Shelby that much."

That he did.

CHAPTER THREE

P etra wandered past the sprawling staircase, her footsteps echoing in the vast building that doubled as the administrative offices of the Hunterdon County Community College. Large windows and French doors lined the back wall that looked out onto a vast pristine lawn. A few young people, students maybe, played soccer on the grass. These adults had their whole lives ahead of them filled with endless possibilities. She clutched the folder with Paige's first semester classes in it. Paige's future would be filled with possibilities too. And way more than hers had ever been.

A bulletin board covered in confetti colored paper took up a large chunk of the side wall. She skimmed over the outdated information from last semester until her gaze rested on a flyer advertising a cooking class—a class anyone could take. Four weeks only. The class started in a few days. Registration was by email.

She looked over her shoulder to make sure no one could see her as she tore the flyer free from its pin in the board. A nonmatriculated class about cooking made a few thoughts buzz free in her head. It wouldn't take up that much time while she was here. She would still be able to pack up the house before her father returned. In fact, the class would be finished before he would be back.

She admonished herself for thinking she needed his approval. But for a split second she was that teenager asking her father to pay for a college degree in culinary arts and watching her future disappear like a magic trick.

The paper stuck to her sweaty grip. It was high time she took control of her life and started making decisions that suited her instead of suiting everyone else. She didn't need approval. She was a middle-aged woman for crying out loud. Still, she folded the paper in quarters and shoved it in her purse.

She hurried back to the parking lot as if she were getting away with something. And maybe she was. She couldn't wait to register. She was alive with glee. But a chuckle stuck in her throat. She wasn't going anywhere.

A fancy red two-door car was parked too close to her driver's door. She didn't know the make or model because all cars looked the same to her, but she was pretty sure the circle emblem on the grill meant expensive. *Figures*. Probably some rich guy being forced to register his kid for school. She couldn't open her door, never mind trying to squeeze inside. She'd have to be Tinkerbell.

The sun glare bounced off the windshield, but an outline of a person behind the wheel could still be made out. She wedged herself between the sideview mirror and her car and knocked on the window. The man, looking at his phone, startled and glared at her.

He mouthed *what* with his palms up.

"You're blocking me in." She pointed to the two cars.

The window lowered. "What did you say?"

With the glass gone, she had a better view of the driver. He filled out most of the space he was sitting in, probably a tall guy. His light-brown hair was parted in a few places, as if his hands had been wrestling up there, and hung in a straight line to his jaw. His unshaven face was a mix of gray and brown and blond. The sleeve of his black faded t-shirt was ripped at the shoulder.

"You're blocking me in. I can't get into my car."

He leaned out the window and looked behind him. He shrugged. "I'll be done in a minute. I have to finish sending this email." The window went back up.

Fury burned through her veins. She marched around the front of the car with its gleaming paint job and knocked on the passenger's window.

He ignored her.

She tried the door and to her surprise the handle lifted. She slid in beside him. The inside of the car was cleaner than hers ever was.

"What the hell are you doing?" He backed against his door, his eyes as wide as a five-pound bag of flour.

His jeans were ripped in several places along his thighs, revealing something black underneath. She didn't want to know what that might be. He had several tattoos along his forearms. This close, she noticed the stains on his shirt too. He probably needed a bath, but the only scent tickling her nose was something cinnamon and very masculine. His gray eyes seemed familiar.

"Will you please move your car now? I have to get home." And sign up for that class before she talked herself out of it.

"Lady, you're nuts. I'll move my car. But you need to get out." He made a move along gesture with his hand. His lips pressed into a thin line.

"You should pay better attention to how you park."

"You should not jump into the cars of strangers. What if I was a killer, setting you up?"

"You wouldn't be very good at your job then. This car stands out like a sore thumb. The cops would find you in no time." She pushed out of the car and stepped out of the way.

He shook his head, but something resembling a smile had unfolded on his face. Without another glance in her direction, he pulled out. The license plate caught her eye. New Jersey. TOPCH3F.

She yanked out the paper from her purse. No mention of any teacher. But that was impossible. No one as well known as Maverick Labraccio would be in Hunterdon County. And she was pretty sure he didn't look like someone living on the streets. But then again... the car and he smelled not only clean, but good.

"Nah. Stuff like that didn't happen here." Just like she had told Ember.

The GPS said his destination was on the left. He still couldn't believe he had agreed to help Avery out, but guilt was funny like that, making him agree to things he would never have otherwise. In a couple of days, he would be the cooking teacher for a bunch of college kids who probably needed a few credits to graduate, but had no interest in real cooking.

This Candlewood Falls town was bigger than he had expected. Farms reached out in every direction, pushing away the houses on acres of land, giving him the sense he could take a deep breath here. The hills dipped and rose in the background of every turn he took. He had passed an apple orchard, a winery, and an alpaca farm.

Mav hit the turn signal at the last second and swung his car onto the long narrow gravel driveway. The commute from his apartment to Candlewood Falls was too far every day. Moving hadn't been a tough decision. He wasn't exactly giving up paradise by relocating. But he would miss Gladys, his neighbor.

He had rented the apartment above a two-door garage which sat at the far back of the driveway. An outside staircase led to the second floor. He passed the owner's house on his left, a small craftsman-style with white clapboard and a little porch on the front. The back had a cement patio with a few planters, two lawn chairs, and a grill. He parked in front of one of the garage bays and got out.

The heat surrounded him like a gang of men he would have to fight his way out of. Too bad this job wasn't at the shore where he might get a sea breeze once in a while. And a chance to see a few beauties in bathing suits before the summer ended.

"I see you made it." An older man hobbled down the back steps of the house and interrupted his thoughts about summer and sand. The sun reflected off the man's bald head. His button-down short-sleeved shirt fit snuggly over his middle, but his light-colored jeans hung loose around his bowlegs.

"You must be Clark. I recognize the voice. It's nice to meet you." He shook hands with his new landlord. Clark had a firm grip and a brightness in his eyes. The smile that spread across Clark's face welcomed him in. He liked the man immediately.

"And you must be the hotshot chef."

"Oh, no. Not me. More of a washed-up cook who's doing a friend a favor." He wasn't sure how much Avery had told Clark about him when she had found the apartment. He hoped it wasn't a whole hell of a lot. Whenever people figured out who he was the questions came tumbling out at rapid speed. *Why did you quit? When are you coming back?* And oh yeah, *we're sorry to hear about your wife. But when are you coming back?* He didn't want to have to talk about his past or explain away his bad choices.

"Your secret is safe with me. I'm not a gossiper. People should keep their noses on their own faces if you get me. Let me show you to your new place." Clark flipped two keys around his finger.

The steps were steep and creaked under their weight. He was glad he hadn't brought that much, carrying anything wider than a suitcase might be a challenge. The apartment had come furnished, a lucky break since his last place had also come that way. He wasn't much into settling down. Not anymore, at least.

Clark gave the door a hard shove. "She sticks in the heat, but a gentle hip-check and she'll give. I took the liberty of turning the a/c on for you. There's a unit up front here in that alcove and one in the bedroom. You'll have no trouble sleeping."

The living space faced the front of the garage with two windows. The pear trees were in full bloom right outside. They provided some privacy and reprieve from the setting sun. The kitchen was toward the back. The one window over the sink looked out on the neighborhood behind them. But the appliances appeared to be on the newer side. A table for two took up most of the floor space in the eating area.

Both the kitchen and living area were met by the alcove Clark had mentioned. The air conditioner ran hard in there, but the space was big enough for an oversized chair and ottoman. A small end table had been tucked in the corner. It reminded him of Shelby's reading nook in their bedroom. He pushed the thought away. If he was going to get through the next four weeks, he didn't need thoughts of Shelby getting in his way.

"This is a nice place," he said, taking it in one more time. Nicer than anywhere he had lived in the past three years.

"The only bath is off the bedroom, but since you're a single guy, I don't think you'll mind much. My last tenants were a couple. Sometimes the young man came running to my place to use the restroom because his young lady was busy with her makeup." Clark choked out a small laugh.

"There's no woman in my life." Relationships weren't for him anymore. He wasn't very good at them—apparently. Though the hellfire earlier today had him doing a double take. When she had jumped into his car, he thought for sure she was going to stab him based on the glare in her blue eyes. If he hadn't parked like a jackass, he might've had more to say to her, but she had been completely in the right. For the first time in longer than he could remember, a woman had rendered him speechless.

"Have you given up on love?" Clark rested the keys on the table.

"I've seen enough rotations around the sun to know that women equal trouble." He would do anything to bring Shelby back. He would gladly go back and tell her to wait for him and not to drive in the rain. He would never cook again if it meant she could be right here giving him holy hell. But the truth was, no matter how much he loved her, it wasn't enough.

"Trust me, son. When you get to be my age, old enough that you've outlived dirt, a man with a straight spine and broad shoulders seems like a boy. My guess is you're somewhere in your early forties. You've barely begun living."

"I never thought about it that way." If he were going to be honest with himself, which was something he approached the way he would a hornet's nest, he hadn't been living at all. Even before Shelby died. Work had consumed him. The restaurant. The television appearances. The interviews. Then after Shelby's accident, he had barely moved from the bed. His best friend had become vodka for a while, until his brother helped him straighten out. Avery's offer had come at the right time. She had probably guessed that.

"Sorry about that not living comment. My wife used to say I rambled at the mouth." A wistful look passed over Clark's face. "I'm right next door if you need anything." Clark stuck out his hand.

He shook again. "I'm not offended, if that's what you mean." He had heard a hell of a lot worse thrown at him than that. Most of it true. He had been an asshole once. Could still be somedays.

"Hey, Clark?" He had a crazy idea.

Clark turned around at the door.

"I saw you had a grill out on your patio."

"Feel free to use it anytime you want. I bought it for a barbeque a few years back, but it doesn't get used much."

"I was wondering if you would join me for dinner?" The whole night lay before him, and he didn't know what he would do with himself. Unpacking would only take about a minute and a half. Work didn't start for two days. He'd had too many nights alone.

"Me?"

"I don't see anyone else here." He smiled and hoped he didn't sound like the jerk he had been accused of being when he ran his restaurant.

Clark's face lit up like that sun poking through the pear trees and leaving ribbons of gold on the floor. "Why, I'd like that. Thank you."

"Great. Now, point me in the direction of the grocery store."

CHAPTER FOUR

P etra tapped her forehead against her parents' bedroom door. Opening a door shouldn't be so difficult. It was just a hollow piece of wood on a hinge. Her fingers fit around the cool glass knob, but they refused the command to turn it. She rubbed the inside of her knuckle against the bevel in the glass just like she did when she was a child and afraid to knock on the door because she didn't like how mad her father became if she woke him. But there was no one on the other side to yell at her or tell her to go away.

She had supported her mother's decision to leave this world on her own terms. In fact, she applauded Ruby who hadn't made a single decision in her life that didn't consider her husband's wishes. Which only infuriated her daughters to no end. Huck had ruled this house with a closed mind and heart. Yet, Mom ignored everyone's protests this time. Petra hadn't bothered to complain or bang her fists. It wasn't her style, and she would make the same decision if she were ever faced with the dilemma.

So, why the hell couldn't she turn the damn knob? "Just go inside. You don't have to move anything. You don't even have the time this morning," she muttered under her breath.

"Who are you talking to?" Paige's appearance in the hallway startled her.

"What? Oh. I was just thinking out loud. I thought you had left." Paige had secured a job at the family's orchard part-time through November from her grandfather. Huck adored Paige, his only grandchild. He had said they were always looking for extra hands this time of year. She suspected that was true, but even if it weren't, Huck would have made it so for Paige—only for Paige.

"In a few minutes. Do you need something in the room?" Paige had secured her hair in a ponytail. She wore an oversized Wilde Orchard t-shirt knotted at her hip and denim cutoff shorts that barely covered the important parts. Paige was tall like Frank, with legs that went on and on. Petra's heart swelled when she saw her daughter, but often deflated as quickly when they argued.

"What makes you say that?"

"Because you're standing there gripping the door." Paige shook her head.

She was, in fact, still holding the knob. She yanked her hand away and rubbed her palm. "Did you eat breakfast? I could whip up some eggs."

"No, thanks. I figured I'd grab a donut at the orchard. Mom, I emailed the school and told them to unregister me." Paige swung her crocheted bag over her shoulder.

"Why would you do that?" She and Paige had fought last night when she handed Paige the folder with the school information. Paige had left the folder on the table and stormed into her room like a category five hurricane. A weather system Petra feared in real life.

"Why won't you listen to me? All those classes and the homework just stress me out. I can't keep up. I don't understand what they're even saying half the time. And what's the point, anyway? I don't even know what I want to be."

"College is a good place to figure it out. Try different things. Join clubs. You never know. Just don't waste time, Paige. You'll blink and be my age." Tears burned the back of her eyes. She found herself fighting off the emotions more and more these days. She blamed it on hormones that had taken over her body. But the emptiness in her chest sometimes, that hole that needed filling, tripped her up.

"I can figure out what I want to do at the orchard and make some money. College will always be there. Don't worry. I won't end up like you."

She tilted up her chin and forced a smile as if Paige's comment hadn't sliced off a piece of her heart. She had never imagined how complicated it would be to raise a child. All the while hoping that someday they would be close. She tried so hard to understand that Paige was angry about the divorce and angry about having to move and angry that Frank didn't have space for her in his new apartment and none of her behavior was personal. But the words stung just the same.

Paige didn't understand that there weren't always second chances. And bad choices made the road so much bumpier.

She brushed past Paige and took the steps two at a time. "A donut isn't breakfast." She grabbed her purse and turned at the door. "I'll see you later. Enjoy your day at work." She closed the door behind her with a snap.

The morning echoed around her. Birds chirped. A car whizzed by out on the road in front of the house. The sun heated up the day and it was barely out of bed. The heat pushed itself against her with force. Her heart ached and the tears threatened. How had she ended up in this spot? She squeezed her eyes shut. She would not allow this day to get off to a bad start. She dug out her phone and dialed Ember.

"Hey, Petra. I was just thinking about you."

"Great minds, and all that. My cooking class starts in a couple of hours. Do you have time for a quick coffee or something?" She didn't want to be alone. And she wanted to get out of there before Paige left. She hopped into her car and pulled out of the driveway.

"Actually, I was about to race over to the orchard. Raf forgot his phone. Do you want to meet me there?"

Something prickly climbed up her throat. If she could see it, the uncomfortable feeling would be green and probably scaley. She was a horrible sister for even entertaining a second of that emotion. Ember deserved all the happiness in the world. But she wanted a tiny piece of it for herself.

"Oh, the orchard. I don't know." She turned at the stop sign in the opposite direction of the orchard. She couldn't go there knowing Paige would be right behind her. They both needed some space.

"It's not that bad. I promise. And Dad isn't there which makes things pleasant. Uncle Silas and Brad are great. Sam is still the same, sweet, nice. Grandpa Skip will be glad to see you. He's getting up there in years."

She hadn't seen her grandfather in forever. Or any of her relatives for that matter. She had stayed away from the orchard and Candlewood Falls because her father had always made that space uncomfortable. The orchard was his. His daughters didn't belong there. He had wanted sons who could work the land and run the business. Ironic that he had insisted she get a business degree when he wouldn't allow her anywhere near his own. And more ironic, he hired Paige in a city minute. She would've loved to have had that version of Huck as her father.

"And you can meet Raf," Ember said.

"I kind of already know Raf." She turned onto the county road that sliced through town and would bring her near the train station. Maybe from there she would head to Main Street and grab a coffee at Green Bean. She wouldn't have to run into anyone there. She'd been gone so long the locals wouldn't remember her. She needed to get gas too. Haffrey's garage always had the best gas prices.

"Now you can meet him as my boyfriend. You're going to love him. He's fantastic. Just this morning, he brought me coffee before I even got out of bed. He knew I went to sleep late and wouldn't want to get up. He's always thinking about what I need. It's incredible."

She was quickly regretting the decision to call Ember. "You know what I just remembered? I have to still buy my textbook for class. I'm so sorry, Ember. Can I take a rain check for breakfast?"

Ember hesitated. "Yeah. Sure. I'll let you get to it. Good luck."

"Thanks. I'll talk to you soon." She ended the call before she could change her mind. She was evil to the core

27

for blowing off her sister, but she wasn't ready for a family reunion and definitely not to meet Raf as the perfect boyfriend. After she had settled in more. Then she'd be ready to paint on a smile and pretend that her life was exactly the way she wanted it.

For now, she'd go to class. She was ready for a new start. Ready for something of her very own.

Mav forced himself down the hall. The shiny tile did nothing to ease the walk. His sneakers squeaked with every step as if to say *your place here isn't right. You don't fit in. Even your shoes are wrong.*

The bulletin boards in different colors and the laughter of students sitting in oversized chairs by the window both seemed off-balance, askew, overcooked if he was going for a bad pun.

Sweat dampened his upper lip, and he wiped it away. He wasn't even sure if he remembered how to cook. How was he going to teach it to a class full of bright-eyed young adults who assumed he had his act together? He doubted the act he had been putting on for the past three years would play out as well in a classroom. College students were savvier than he was. They would see right through the thin mask he tried to wear.

He checked the number on the piece of paper and read the plaques beside each door as the numbers outside the classroom rose. Of course, his room was the last one on the right. He glanced over his shoulder at where he had come from. Not far enough. And yet too far as well.

The night Shelby had died, he had been elbow deep in

a clogged sink in the kitchen of his restaurant—Labraccio's. He had told her he would be home in time for the fundraiser she had been planning. But the place was packed with guests and his sous chef had burned his hand only minutes before. He knew he should leave. The weather was terrible and Shelby didn't see well at night to drive. But she was stubborn and so was he. He couldn't just walk out when the dirty water in the sink spilled over the side in waves, crashing on the red tile floor and making a huge puddle and hazard. His waitress, Tess, nearly landed on her ass as she plowed through it. A clog would be a quick fix. But it wasn't. And then Jon was shoving his hand in a bucket of ice and screaming every curse word known to man. Shelby would have to wait. She would understand.

But she hadn't. At all. She had left him a voicemail calling him an asshole and saying she was leaving for the fundraiser and leaving him too. He hadn't heard the voicemail until after the police had come to the restaurant to tell him about her accident.

On a deep breath, he opened the classroom door, hoping for another five or ten minutes to get settled before the students began filtering in, but his luck wouldn't hold out. Instead, three students, all of whom seemed to be well above the average college-aged student, sat at desks that filled the front of the room. They each had chosen a random spot far away from the others. They probably didn't know each other.

At the back of the room were three mini kitchens each with shiny new stainless-steel appliances and all the cabinets they would need. Avery had told him the cabinets were filled with measuring cups, bowls, and top-of-the-line utensils. There were two rolling steel racks positioned to the side, filled with dried goods in plastic containers. Avery had been right about the workspace. He had everything he needed.

The woman in front turned as he entered. Her dark-brown hair fell straight but at her shoulders turned to soft waves. Her full lips were pressed into a straight line, but when realization dawned in her blue eyes, those beautiful lips turned down. She cocked her head and raised a thick brow.

"You," she said.

"Apparently. Nice to see you again." What else could he say? Though it was the truth. He could look at her all day. She was the most beautiful woman he had ever seen.

He glanced away and suddenly wished he'd worn a shirt with a few less wrinkles.

"Do you two know each other?" the older man with a full head of white hair streaked with a few strands of black and soft olive skin at his jawline said.

"No," she said.

"We met in the parking lot," he said at the same time.

"I didn't believe it when I heard, but you're really Maverick Labraccio," the other woman, probably in her late sixties with short blond hair and rings on every finger, said. "I'm Cristina Urban, by the way. My friends call me Titi. I'm so excited to be here." She held her hands out palms up and smiled. Her bright-pink lipstick bled into the creases around her mouth.

"Hello…" The expectant gazes tangled his words in his mouth. He took a deep breath. "I'll be your teacher for the next few weeks."

He dropped his phone and the piece of paper on the

desk. He probably should have brought a notebook or his laptop, not that he used that much, but at least he might have the appearance of knowing what he was doing.

The beautiful woman gripped a notebook with both hands. She had a pencil and two pens lined up neatly at the top of the desk. Her back was as straight as a cutting board. She raised her hand.

"You don't need to raise your hand." He hoped he forced a smile on his face, but by the quizzical look she gave him, he had probably failed. He didn't want this place to be formal. He just wanted to get to the end of the four weeks.

She shifted in her seat. The silver bracelet slid down her arm. "Well, okay, but we are in a classroom. Anyway, it's a dumb question, but will we begin cooking right away?"

He hadn't planned out a schedule. He figured he spend the first class getting to know the students a little and see if they even wanted to cook. He kind of hoped they were all just here for some credits. Then he could wing the whole thing.

"Why don't we wait until the rest of the class shows up, and then I'll get into the plan." He should have had that second cup of coffee. Maybe he could skip out for a few minutes and grab one. He had passed some kind of café inside the front doors.

"This is the whole class. Didn't they tell you?" the man with the white hair said.

"Who is they?" Avery hadn't mentioned what his final enrollment was. He hadn't bothered to ask either.

"Admissions. I called yesterday to confirm the class

would begin. They told me yes because you had reached the minimum number of students allowed," the man said.

"I guess it's lucky then that I registered. I just did it two days ago. I wasn't going to, but my friend talked me into it," Titi, with the rings on her fingers, said.

A class of only three students? He had quit his job at the warehouse and left his apartment to relocate to some town in the middle of New Jersey for three students? Hadn't the school advertised who was teaching? He knew he wasn't as popular as he was three years ago. The world of fame and food waited for no one, but hell, he had been on top of that world once. He figured a few people would be here just to meet him. He wasn't going to force himself to act like a chef again for three students. "Would you all excuse me for a second?"

He grabbed his phone and went into the hallway, making sure to close the door behind him. He pulled up Avery's number and waited for her to answer.

"Hi, Mav. Is everything okay? Please tell me you're at the class." Her voice was rushed and shrill.

"Yes, Avery. I'm here. You neglected to tell me that I only had three students. And they're all older than me, well, except for one. But these aren't real students. You're going to have to find someone else." He paced away from the door.

"Mav, take a deep breath and put your ego in check. You weren't the original teacher, remember? I'm sure if I had more time to advertise you properly, the class would have been filled. Besides, a smaller class will make it easier for them to cook. That's what those very real paying students want to do. Don't forget that."

"I just expected…" What had he expected? A bunch of groupies wanting his autograph? He hadn't even wanted to come here, and here he was all tied up in knots because no one was interested in him as a chef. He had fallen from his throne and whether he liked it or not, he missed being in it.

"Does it really matter how many students are there? You're getting paid the same. Please just teach them. You're a good teacher."

"How would you know that?" He wasn't so sure. How could she be?

"Because Shelby told me. I'm hanging up. Don't be such a baby and go teach." She ended the call.

He stared at the phone and forced himself not to throw it down the hall. He wasn't a baby. He wasn't ready to go back in the kitchen with other people. He had never thought of himself as a teacher. When a new person worked in his kitchen, he was always happy to help them, show them how he liked things done. That wasn't teaching exactly because if they couldn't keep up, they were fired. He can't fire these three. Could he?

The door opened and the beautiful woman poked her head out. "Is everything all right?"

He glanced at his phone as if the answers were there, then shoved it in his pocket. "Of course, why wouldn't it be?"

"Because you disappeared. We're wondering when you're going to get started. The class is only an hour. The first twenty minutes have gone by already."

A control freak and an overachiever. Just what he needed. Okay, he would show the pretty lady how it was done. He'd find a way to make her stay on her toes. He had no idea how he would do that, if he could even pull it off anymore. Every time he thought about running another kitchen, he broke out in a sweat and his bowels cramped. He had no right to do what he loved when it had killed his wife.

But he couldn't allow Avery to lose her job because of him. He had been the reason too many people were disappointed. He was pretty sure he'd disappoint those three people in that classroom too.

"Well? Are you coming?" she said.

"You shouldn't frown so much."

"Excuse me?" She stepped into the hall. The door closed on a swish.

"If you keep looking at me like I kicked a golden retriever puppy, that crease between your brow is going to stay there." He made a hand gesture between his eyes.

A hint of a smile touched the corner of her lips. The crease lightened and his heart did something that could either be fluttering or he was about to have a heart attack and really screw up his day.

"Never mind my eyebrows. The class is waiting for you." She reached for the doorknob.

"Okay. Okay. Point made. But for the record, I don't kick puppies."

She glanced over her shoulder, the smile gone. "I certainly hope not. But you do think the world revolves around you."

"No, I don't."

"Really? Next time you're on the phone outside your classroom, don't speak so loudly. There might only be three of us in there, and only one who knew who you were, but we're real students, I assure you, sir." She yanked open the door and left him in the hall—picking his jaw up off the floor.

CHAPTER FIVE

P etra returned to her seat. She hadn't known what to expect when she arrived. The classroom was more like the set of a cooking challenge show than a standard classroom and her heart had soared when she walked through the three sets of kitchens. Her own kitchen had been functional, but not pretty. And the kitchen in her parents' house was just old—but her mother's oven worked like a champ.

She was relieved to find out that there were only three students. One kitchen for each of them. Had there been ten or twenty students, they would all have been crammed in the back, having to share and wait their turns just like when she was a child and she had to wait her turn for her mother's attention. This way was much better.

But their teacher—the one and only Maverick Labraccio—didn't seem to think so. The minute his voice carried through the walls, she searched him on the internet to find out where he'd been hiding. Three years ago, he was clean-cut with a dazzling smile. And why not?

He had it all. She hadn't bothered to click on any of the articles when she had decided to go out in the hall and see if he was ever going to begin teaching.

"Maybe he isn't coming back," the man with the very nice head of salt-and-pepper hair said. "This isn't a good sign. I'm going to ask for my money back." He stood. The metal legs of his chair scraped against the linoleum.

"Oh, give him a chance." The woman called Titi waved her hand in the air. Her rings caught the glint of the fluorescent light. "He's probably used to having his ego stroked. Head chef in a five-star restaurant. A short run television show. He's been featured in every cooking magazine and even hit *People*'s list of sexy men. He was probably expecting a full house." Titi tsked and shook her head.

"How long should we give him?" She had expected him to follow her right in, but he had only stared at her with his mouth gaping open. She ran a finger up and down between her eyebrows. Was she frowning too much? Probably. But she would never admit that to one of the sexiest men alive. Not that she believed that.

"Why don't we get to know each other until he comes back. Like I said, I'm Titi. I've always wanted to take a cooking class. I'm a terrible cook. Honestly, the worst. Hopefully, I'll come out of this at least able to boil water. How about the two of you?"

She and the man shared a look, but they both stayed quiet. It seemed he wasn't in the mood to share either. She wasn't ready to say she was recently divorced, that she moved back into her parents' house or that she had taken this class to keep her out of said house so she wouldn't have to be faced with removing all traces of her mother.

"Oh, all right," the man said. "My name is Nicholas. My friends call me Niko. I'm only taking this class because my wife signed me up for it. I'm recently retired and she wants me out of the house. Says I'm getting in her way."

"Oh, I'm sure that's not true," she said. She had no way of knowing any such thing, but it seemed like the right thing to say. If she had ever tried to sign Frank up for a class without his knowledge, he wouldn't have gone anyway. Niko's wife probably knew deep down he wanted to take a cooking class, but would never register on his own. That idea warmed the center of her chest a little. She would love to have someone be that thoughtful with her.

Titi and Niko stared at her. She glanced at the door to see if their leader would return and save her from speaking, but he continued to pace on the other side. She didn't want to alienate the first new people she had met in Candlewood Falls, but she wasn't ready for budding relationships of any kind. She took a deep breath for courage.

"My name is Petra… Wilde." That was taking some getting used to. She wanted her maiden name back and took it the second the ink was dry on the divorce papers. Her married name had never felt right on her lips. "I love to cook. In fact, I had wanted to study culinary arts a long time ago, but I wasn't brave enough. I'm not sure I'm much braver now, but this is a start. I'd like to see where the class takes me." And by the looks of Mr. Labraccio, nowhere. She bit back the bitter taste of disappointment. Maybe Niko had the right idea about getting a refund.

The door opened and Maverick barreled back in. "Okay, sorry about that. So, here's the deal. Starting tomorrow I'm going to work you the way I worked with every person in my kitchen. Things will move fast. You had better keep up. And if you think you can't, then see if the school will refund your money." His hands moved at the same animated speed as his words.

"What do you mean *things will move fast?*" Titi squirmed in her seat.

"Think of it as on the job training."

"I don't understand," Niko said, leaning on the corner of the desk.

"You'll see tomorrow. I have to go pick up some things for us. I'm letting you out a little early today, but don't be late tomorrow." He pointed at each one of them.

She wanted to remind him that he had been the last one to arrive today, but she had said enough when it came to this man. She resisted the urge to touch the spot between her brows again.

"Count me in." Niko tapped the desk with his knuckles.

"I can't wait," Titi said.

"Aren't you going to start with the basics? Like how to chop or sauté or something?" She wasn't prepared to jump into the deep end and just whip up some fancy meal by some famous chef. Sure, she could cook, loved to do it, even had a few meals her family requested, but this class was supposed to be her stepping stone to something bigger than what she was now. She couldn't just skip to the end. She needed guidance. Assurance even that she knew what she was doing.

"It's going to be sink or swim in here. Just like in a real kitchen. I don't know what everyone's goals are for this class, but if you ever want to cook professionally, no one is going to hold your hand. There's no time to be scared when people want their food."

"Come on, Petra, this will be fun. Who cares about the basics?" Titi said.

She didn't know if this class was for her after all. Her heart sunk. She had wanted to come here, learn a few things, dip her toe in and see how the water was. This guy wanted them to be Olympians out of the gate. She needed to take her time. She had enough pressure with her mother's issues. She pushed out of the chair. Maybe the school had a different class she could take.

"You aren't leaving already, are you?" Maverick Labraccio said. His name rolled around in her mouth, but she wouldn't dare let the taste of it leave her tongue. She would try them out later, when she was alone. This man's presence unsettled her in a way that made her tingle and twitch at the same time.

She pointed at the clock. "Class is over. I have somewhere else to be."

Well, that went poorly. The beautiful woman with the name Petra was probably marching straight to admissions and asking for a full refund. He could imagine her using words like arrogant, in the wrong place, no business teaching. If she dropped, then the class would be canceled; he would lose the job he needed now, and Avery would lose hers too. He should have pulled himself together and not ranted about being misled. For a split second, he had thought he was important again. The old sensation of wanting his kitchen his way had clouded his brain like a bad drug. He hadn't even noticed the change in him until Petra had stuck her head out the door.

His other two students left, leaving him alone in the classroom. The clock on the wall ticked away each second, reminding him time was not promised. He had tried not to waste his, but these last three years had him in a tailspin he couldn't control.

And then there was Petra. She would make this job harder on him. He wouldn't be able to skate through the next four weeks like he had planned with her looking over his shoulder. He would have to show the pretty lady how strenuous a kitchen could be. Then maybe that chip on her shoulder would slip a little.

He hadn't noticed a ring on her finger, but she probably ran a tight ship at home, telling her poor husband what to do and when. Not the kind of woman for him. Not that he was looking. Women equaled trouble. Or worse, he equaled trouble for them.

Outside, the sun baked the asphalt of the parking lot. The bottom of his sneakers cooked with each step, making his feet hot. His phone vibrated against his hip. He dug it out of his pocket and read his brother's name across the screen. He debated on answering, but if he didn't, Sebastian would just keep calling.

"Hey, Sebastian." He hadn't spoken to his brother in weeks. They usually did their own things, going in opposite directions. That was fine for him, but recently Bash wanted to be close. Like they were when they were kids.

"Mav, how's the new gig going?" He boasted that voice he used to schmooze clients. Bash was always on. Mav wasn't sure if Bash even had an off switch.

"So far so good." He would save Bash the epic fail of

his first class. Bash never failed at anything. He had been the golden child. Where Mav was a different story entirely, until the restaurant fame. But it hadn't lasted. No surprise there where their father was concerned.

"That's great. So that class of yours got off to a good start. I'm glad. It's good you got back in the kitchen."

"It's not exactly the same thing. But the class was okay." He forgot where he parked his car. He must've come out of the building and gone in the wrong direction. He circled back while Bash kept talking.

"I was wondering if you were free Friday night for dinner. I thought I would take a drive and see this Candlewood Falls for myself," Bash said.

"Not much to see." Something was up. A town like Candlewood Falls would never appeal to his brother who preferred the fast-moving cities that stayed open all night long.

He cut through the center of the parking lot by moving between cars. Coming out between an Accord and a pickup, he spotted Petra dumping her purse on the ground. He should turn and go back the other way before she noticed him and gave him more of her opinions.

"I need a getaway for a few days. I can't be at home." Bash's voice distracted him from watching Petra.

"Decided you'd slum it with me instead of taking Jess to an exotic beach someplace?" He meant for the words to come out light and easy, but they fell flat and tasted sour. Watching Bash and Jess have it all was hard to swallow most days. He should be happy for his brother; it hadn't been Bash's fault that his own life fell apart in so many ways. Bash had been the one who had tried to help him in the beginning. But he hadn't wanted help. He still didn't.

"Jess is moving out," Bash said pragmatically.

He stopped in his tracks, kicking a rock as he did it. Petra turned at that moment and saw him. An emotionless mask fell over her face.

"Hey, I'm sorry. What happened?"

"Some other guy with more money than me happened. I don't want to talk about it."

"Yes, come. You can sleep on the couch." He couldn't believe Bash and Jess were breaking up. They had what looked like the perfect relationship. Two very independent and successful people who lived together, never complaining about how much the other one worked, always supporting the other's career. Neither wanted children. Their schedules were packed every weekend with the kind of social events that made most people drool.

"I was only thinking dinner."

"Save it. This is me you're talking to. The place is small, but we'll manage. I'll text you the address. I'm sorry to do this, but I have to run. I'll call you tonight. You can tell me all about what happened."

"Yeah. Okay. Great. See ya." Bash ended the call.

He took a slow step toward Petra who was throwing her hands in the air. "Do you need any help?"

She glanced at her belongings on the hot ground then back at him. "No, thank you." She gathered her things, including that notebook from class, and shoved them back in her very large bag. She stood by the practical gray sedan that he had blocked in the other day, her gaze never leaving his.

"Are you sure you're all right? Did you lose something? I could help you look." He had gotten off to a bad start with her. He wanted to make up for it. He used to be good with people. Not the way Bash was, but he had a full social calendar too once.

"I am perfectly fine." She waved her hand in front of her as if to say *keep walking, pal. Nothing to see here.* The same gesture he had given her. He didn't like being on the receiving end of it.

"You can't find your keys, right?" He should leave this woman alone. She clearly didn't want anything to do with him. Sticking his nose where it didn't belong would only get it cut off.

She slumped against the car. The fight drained out of her. "I swore I put them in my purse. I've checked every pocket twice, and I tossed everything out as you saw. It's just been that kind of day."

"What kind?" He really should stop talking. She didn't want him there. But he wanted to make that adorable crease between her brow go away.

"The not good kind. My day started off... well, never mind that. And now you're going to turn our class into some kind of advanced placement thingy which I hadn't signed up for. I just need my stupid keys." She scooped her hair away from her face with a loud sigh.

"I do want to teach."

"Oh, please, Mr. Labraccio. You didn't even try and hide how upset you were because the class is so small. I suppose someone like you can't be bothered with just three adult students trying to better themselves. You were probably hoping for a classroom of twenty-somethings who hung on your every word."

She had him all wrong and it stung. "Did you read that article *Cooking Now* had written a few years ago? They made me out to be a playboy chef, but that isn't true."

"I have no idea what you're talking about. I don't pay attention to celebrities. But since you seem to think I've read articles about you and drawn my conclusions, then you must be the arrogant chef I assumed you were."

"Hang on. I'm getting this all wrong. That's not what I meant."

"Whatever. If you'll excuse me, I need to make a call so I can get out of here." She pulled out her phone and tapped at the screen.

"Let me take you."

Her gaze snapped up from the phone. "Why would I do that?"

"Whoever you're texting will have to come out and get you. I'm already here. And I want you to enjoy class."

"I won't be there. This class was a dumb idea on my part." She searched through her bag again. This time she pulled out a hair tie and secured her hair off her face.

"You're going to quit?" He couldn't allow that to happen.

"That's what I said." She shook her head with a smirk and an eye roll.

"Let me give you a ride and try to talk you into staying."

"Why would I let you talk me into staying? You don't even like me."

"Not true." He was liking this banter a little too much. Her feisty personality ignited something in him. He bet she had a good laugh too. "Without you, I'll lose my job and so will my friend who organized this class. I need every student." He tried to look humble, but didn't know if it worked. He really did need her to stay in the class. He'd beg if he had to.

"I'll take the ride."

"Great." He tried to open the door for her, but she brushed him away.

He slid in beside her. The sweet clean smell of lemon icing floated off her and reached for him. He rubbed his sweaty palms on his shorts. He couldn't remember the last time he drove a woman in his car. He just wished this one would smile a little.

"Mr. Labraccio, can you drop me at the Green Bean? I'm meeting my sister there." She strangled the life out of her bag, twisting the handles the way she was.

"I don't know where that is. And call me Mav."

"Main Street. I'll direct you." She readjusted her ponytail and shifted in her seat as if no spot was comfortable.

"Mav." He stole another glance at her. Her back was straight again as if leaning against the seat might wrinkle her. She pressed her knees together, and her hands still clutched her bag.

"What?" She stared at him with wide eyes.

"I'll direct you, Mav. Please call me Mav. Anything else is too formal." He tried to smile, to let her in on his stupid attempt at a joke.

She bent her head and laughed, relaxing against the seat finally. Score for the out-of-practice weird guy. Immediately he wondered why her laughing at his joke was so important. Enough that he missed what she had said next.

"Turn here." She pointed to the left almost hitting him in the face. "You're going to miss the street. I guess you're very new to Candlewood Falls."

"It's that obvious?"

"Everyone knows where Main Street is who lives here or who has lived here. Candlewood Falls isn't exactly a big town. Make a left and go over the bridge. Green Bean will be farther down on the corner."

He drove over the bridge and admired the red mill with its small waterfall. Main Street was something right out of a novel. Small shops with colorful storefronts welcoming in visitors. People walked down the street, pointing and stopping to look in windows. Cars lined the street on both sides. Trees had been planted strategically along the sidewalk. Or maybe Main Street had grown up around the trees that had once been here.

"Is your sister already here?" He found a place to park on the block after the coffee shop. He didn't want Petra to leave just yet. She was like a recipe he couldn't get just right, but wanted to keep at it until he did. He couldn't have her hate him off the bat.

"I wasn't honest with you. I'm not meeting her." She ducked her head again.

"Oh." He had that coming, didn't he? He had behaved like a jerk earlier, making her and the others think he was too important for them, when that was the furthest thing from the truth.

"I'm sorry I lied. I'm not ready to show a strange man where I live even if he's my new teacher. Please understand."

"You're worried about me seeing where you live, but you weren't worried about jumping into the car of a stranger the other day?" She was completely unexpected. He was intrigued.

Her full laugh filled the car. "Yeah, I'm sorry about that. When I need something done, I just go for it. To a fault, unfortunately."

"I understand that. I think. But I wouldn't make it a habit. Not everyone is safe."

"Now you sound like my father."

"Sorry. Not going for that. Can I buy you a coffee?"

"Oh. No, thank you. I appreciate the ride, though." Her hand was on the door.

"How will you get home?"

"I will call my sister after all. She'll come and get me."

"But you didn't give me a chance to convince you to stay in class."

"I'll stay." Her lips broke open into a smile, wide and bright. The light danced in her eyes. She was good at smiling.

"That was easier than I thought. Thanks. I appreciate the help in keeping my job."

"I'm doing this for me. Not you. I'm sticking with my decision to take the class. Even if you can't teach. I hope for our sake you'll learn how to and fast." She pushed the door open. The heat swooped in and covered them.

He reached for her wrist. "I won't let you down. I promise." A promise he should never make. Had no right to make and wished he could take back. But it was out there, stuck between them.

"We'll see. Thank you for the ride." She closed the door with a soft thud. He waited until he couldn't see her in the rearview mirror any longer before pulling out into traffic again.

She had doubted him and his declaration. Maybe she was right about him. He and his promises couldn't be trusted. But he wanted to prove her wrong. Badly.

CHAPTER SIX

Petra didn't dare look behind her, but she wanted to. Instead, she put one foot in front of the other and some distance between Mav's fancy car and her.

She couldn't believe she had taken a ride from him. She could have called Ember to come get her, but his stormy gray eyes were warm, unlike the first time when she got in his car. He was delicious-looking in his black t-shirt. The short sleeves stretched over his biceps. The messy hair was growing on her too. Her fingers wanted to take a run through his long locks and see how soft they were.

She had clutched her tote bag the entire ride to keep from reaching out and brushing her hand against his arm like a lovesick girl trying to flirt. Not that she wanted to flirt with her sexy teacher. Oh boy, she could not become the cliché student with a crush on her professor. How worn out was that story? And not for her. She was there to cook food. The rest of the time she would be packing up her mother's belongings.

She pulled on the door to the Green Bean with too much force and almost went flying backward. The cool air from inside rushed out to grab her and she leaned into it. The day was hotter than a tea kettle whistling in the wind. Or maybe it was just her and her recent encounter with a man.

The Green Bean had barely changed since her last visit here. The strong aroma of freshly brewed coffee still filled the air. People sat at the same small round tables deep in conversation or with their noses inches from their laptops. She couldn't be sure, but she thought Malbec River and Caleb Ransom were at the table in the corner talking like a couple of old hens.

Caleb said something funny and Malbec high-fived him. Malbec's family owned the town winery. He had returned to Candlewood Falls last fall and ended up falling in love and staying. Caleb had been wrongly accused of killing her uncle SJ. Caleb had spent some time in jail, but had been released and also last fall had fallen in love with her cousin Brooklyn.

Her mother had given her all the town gossip back then. Her heart ached for her mother whom she would never see again. The phone would never ring with her mother on the other end, ready to spill all her town news. She wished she could call her mom now and tell her about her little encounter with Mav.

A young barista smiled at her from behind the counter. A glass case filled with sugary treats begged her to take a peek.

"Hi. I'd like an iced coffee with skim milk please. And one of these blueberry lemon scones." She had never had breakfast and her heart had pounded hard, burning up calories when she couldn't find her keys and then again sitting next to Mav.

She paid for her goodies and took a spot by the window. Malbec and Caleb had left while she was ordering. She would have to give Brooklyn a call and catch up.

She needed to text Ember and get a ride or she'd be walking back to the house and that would take forever. Taking a sip of the coffee and a bite of the scone, she sent the text.

Any chance you're around?

Running errands. Ember was always on the move. She barely sat still. Petra could not keep up with that pace even when they were kids.

I'm stuck at the coffee shop. Can I get a ride?

Be there soon.

She sent a heart emoji in response and put the phone on the table.

Her phone pinged. Paige had sent a text. She wasn't sure if she wanted to read it. Would it be a continuation of their argument this morning? But guilt or motherly responsibility had her picking up the phone.

Hi, Mom. Met a friend at work. Going to grab something to eat after. Will be home later.

Does this person have a name? They had barely settled in and Paige had made a friend.

She was glad for that. She wanted Paige to like it in Candlewood Falls because most likely this town would be their home for a while.

Junior. Picks apples.

Her mind created a list of questions she wanted to fire off, but she stifled each and every one of them. She would give Paige the space she craved, and truth be told, she

51

craved the space as well. She almost wished her ex had a spare bedroom for Paige. Even having the last few weeks of summer to herself would have been like a vacation.

Don't be late. She hit send and immediately wished she hadn't. If Paige had been away at college, she would have no idea what her daughter was doing. She was trying to connect more with her, and only managing to do the opposite. She was certain, without looking, that Paige would not respond to her last text.

The door swung open again. Ember came in and searched the space until their gazes met. Her sister's face lit up. Petra jumped from her seat. They hadn't seen each other in person since her return to town. Ember had been so busy and she had been avoiding her sister and her new life like a jealous child. They gripped each other in a tight hug, rocking back and forth. The smell of sugar and vanilla clung to Ember.

"I've missed you," Ember said against her head.

"Me too. Us being together is the one saving grace about this whole thing." She would have come to Candlewood Falls just to be with Ember if she had only asked. Since the divorce, Petra was lonely. Not that Frank had ever been much company.

Ember pulled back. "Petra, it's all going to work out. When I first came to town in April, I felt the same way you do about Mom. But this is what she wanted. I think she's brave."

She nodded. The words stuck in the web of emotions strangling her. If she opened her mouth, she feared she would cry. Crying here would be a disaster. Her mother was brave. She was the one who was too frightened to do what she was supposed to.

Someone cleared their throat. She peered around Ember.

"Oh. Sorry." Ember jumped back to include the tall male with black hair and bright smile. His work shirt was stained in places with dirt. His jeans were faded and torn at the knees. She didn't need an introduction to the man who had stolen her sister's heart, but one was coming.

"Petra, this is Raf. Raf, my older sister." Ember bounced on her toes. She was as excited as she used to get on Christmas morning.

"Hi," Raf said and turned to Ember. "Babe, I've known your sister since high school."

"I know, but now you're *my* Raf and I wanted a new introduction." Ember looked between them with expectancy.

She didn't have the heart to burst Ember's bubble. "It's nice to see you again, Raf. Thanks for coming." She stuck out her hand and Raf slid his firm grip into hers.

"Nice to see you too for the first time ever. I've forgotten all about the Wilde sisters who roamed the hallways of Candlewood Falls High, ignoring the likes of me and my brothers." Raf laughed full and long. Ember swatted at him.

"You're impossible," Ember said.

Raf beamed at her sister. That ugly, mangy green monster sat on her shoulder. She wanted to flick it into oblivion. Instead, she reached for her iced coffee and scone. "Hey, do you know where I can get another key?"

"Have you checked all your pockets?" Ember said.

"I thought so." She hadn't told Maverick that she had been distracted the first time she had looked. Frank had sent a text saying he didn't want Paige to come for a few weeks. He had things to do. As if that explained it all. She had been spitfire mad. "Maybe I'll look again."

She checked each pocket with care this time, including the smaller one on the outside with the zipper. "Oh boy." She held up the black key fob.

"That's good news," Raf said.

"I feel pretty stupid. I'm sorry to make you come out here." It wasn't just Frank that had her forgetting where she placed things. When Maverick had appeared between the two cars like an apparition, his very male presence had jarred thoughts she was sure were dormant. She hadn't even bothered to look in her purse a third time.

"How did you get here?" Raf scratched at his jaw.

"She took a ride from her teacher." Ember wagged her eyebrows. "It's something out of an old eighties movie."

"Stop it. He was there. I didn't know what to do and didn't know if you could come right away." She had enjoyed the ride. He was charming even if he was arrogant and self-absorbed.

"Are you in a hurry? Raf and I thought we'd sit and catch up with you." Ember slipped a hand around Raf's arm.

"I don't have anywhere to be. Paige is hanging out with a friend after work."

"I saw her today. She was doing a great job on the register," Raf said. "I can keep an eye on her for you, if you want. Just to make sure she's settling in okay. There's a lot going on now. It can be overwhelming when the customers start demanding things."

"That would be nice." Paige might not appreciate the gesture, but she wouldn't mention it. Not after the whole registering her for class thing. Maybe since this was her aunt's boyfriend, Paige would welcome the attention. As long as it wasn't her idea, Paige didn't object as loudly.

"Who's the friend?" Ember said.

"Someone named Junior. I didn't ask for more details. I'm sure she wouldn't have given them willingly." She took the chair she had just vacated. Ember sat beside her. Raf remained standing.

"Junior?" His eyes narrowed and he scratched his jaw again. "Junior Ramirez? One of my summer pickers?"

"I don't know. Oh, wait. She did say he picked apples. You know him then."

"It's none of my business, but she might not want to spend a whole lot of time with him. Junior is a bit of a player with the young ladies." Raf shoved his hands in his back pockets. "I've seen him several times with different girls. I mean women. Sorry." He held his hands in surrender.

"Don't mind him." Ember patted his arm. "He's a lovable chauvinist."

"So, he gets around, in other words?" Her motherly instincts kicked into overdrive. She didn't want her impressionable daughter hanging with a young man who played the field. Paige hadn't had a serious boyfriend yet. She wasn't used to relationships. She would never see this Junior Ramirez coming.

"He started with us in May right after school had let out. He goes to NYU or something for horticulture... whatever." Raf waved a hand in the air. "Since then, he's dated easy five different girls. Brad had said something to him about it because Junior has brought the young ladies to the orchard. Brad didn't want anything coming down on Junior or us if something went south."

"Why does he bring them there?" Petra said.

"It's usually his first date. They pick apples. He gives them a bit of a tour. Junior told Brad to mind his own business."

"He means our cousin Brad," Ember said.

"Yes, sister. I know who he means. Brad is the vice president of operations. I listen when Dad talks about the orchard."

"Really?" Ember's brow line shot up.

"It's the bakery that fascinates me. I always told Dad he should have a café there too. Someplace where the customers can get a cute sandwich or salad with their apple cider donut. He never listens to me, though." She had brought it up a dozen times as far back as college, which was a lifetime ago. Her father always pushed her ideas away as if they weren't worth it. He had never given much credence to his daughters' desires. He had his own ideas about how they should live their lives.

"You should mention the café idea to Brad sometime," Raf said. "He's always looking for ways to expand the business. I'm going to grab a coffee. Can I get you ladies anything?"

Ember put in her request. She held up her iced coffee and her scone. Raf sauntered off to the counter.

"What do you think of him?" Ember leaned across the table as if they were conspirators in a devilish plan. Her eyes sparkled and her smile was impish.

"He seems very nice. And he's handsome. I'm happy for you." She really was, but that didn't change the fact she could barely remember being in love. That anticipation in her belly when Frank would walk into a room. Too much time and too many disappointments had doused that flame.

Ember grabbed her hand. "He has brothers. I could introduce you."

"No. I don't have time for that. I'm here to pack up Mom's things, take my little cooking class, and then figure out my next move."

"But you'll stay in Candlewood Falls, right? I need you here."

"Let's not worry about that right now." Nyx had offered for her to come and live in Nashville with her too, when the house was done. But starting over in a new state where she knew no one except her sister who toured the world didn't have any appeal. Candlewood Falls was familiar and would most likely win out.

"You don't have to think it to death. This is a great town with a lot of opportunities. Just say you'll stay."

Raf returned with more than just coffee and saved her from responding.

"Look who's here." Raf flashed a quick smile.

Standing next to him was their very tall, very built cousin. His hair was to his shoulders. His skin was tanned from working out in the sun. And he had a very intricate tree tattoo on his arm. He sported a five-o'clock shadow and his faded t-shirt and jeans had a well-worn look. If she didn't know him, she would probably cross the street when she saw him coming. There was something a little menacing about Brad Wilde.

"Hi, Ember. Hey, Petra. When did you get back in town?" Brad leaned in and kissed her on the cheek. She caught a whiff of apples and fresh air.

"Hi, Brad. Just recently. It's nice to see you." She was glad to be around family. She would have to be sure to visit with all her cousins while she was here. She and her sisters often avoided their cousins because usually every holiday Huck had embarrassed them by starting a fight with his brothers. Only Brad's father, Silas, could put up with her father. It was easier to keep a distance than subject herself to the sideways glances and awkward communications.

Ember slapped her arm. "Ask him about the café at the orchard."

She rubbed the spot where Ember's hand had left a sting. Her mouth clamped shut. She tried to give Ember a glare that said to stop talking, that she wasn't about to discuss some idea that had only hit the air a few moments before. She had no plans, no thoughts, no ideas, nothing but her sister always willing to jump off a bridge without looking below.

"What café? We don't have a café," Brad said.

"Tell him what we were talking about." Ember gritted her teeth and nodded, implying she should say something.

She had nothing to say. She would not talk about a passing thought. Ember was out of her mind, bringing this up now. "I don't know what she means."

Ember rolled her eyes. "I meant the café she needs to open."

"At the orchard?" Brad said. He glanced off as if picturing a café somewhere on the orchard, then looked at her. "That's not a bad idea. I've thought about it over the years. We could expand the bakery to include real food. Text me. We'll set up a meeting. I've got to run. See you guys." Brad grabbed his order at the counter and left with a wave.

"What did you go and do that for?" It was her turn to slap Ember.

"Oh, boy. Sister fight. I'll wait for you two at the truck. Take your time." Raf followed in Brad's recent footsteps.

"What are you so upset about? Brad likes the idea. It's perfect for you. And it's a reason for you to stay in Candlewood Falls."

She pushed out of the chair hard enough to almost knock it over. "How many times do I have to tell you that I'm not like you? I'm not going to jump into some business I never even gave a thought about just like that. I don't even want to own a café or run one, or whatever. I'm still trying to figure things out. Stop interfering where you aren't wanted." She grabbed her purse and pushed past Ember.

"When are you going to start living your life?" Ember called after her. Some of the patrons turned and stared at them.

She swallowed the lump in her throat. "When you stop trying to live it for me."

"Petra, wait."

But she didn't. She pushed out into the afternoon heat with fire in her veins. How dare Ember set her up like that? She glanced around for her car and then remembered it was still at the school. She would have to walk back there and get it. Maybe by then she wouldn't be mad enough to strangle Ember. Or maybe she still would.

CHAPTER SEVEN

Mav handed Vinny, the butcher, the cash. "Thanks."

"Enjoy the flat irons." Vinny, in his green polo shirt and threadbare apron, handed him change.

He had driven around town after he dropped off Petra. He hadn't liked the way things ended between them. He was convinced she didn't believe him that he would show up to class able to teach them. It was as if she could see right through the thin veil of promises he had been making to himself and everyone else for a long time. Long before he had lost Shelby. He had been so driven back then. Driven to make his career the most important thing in his life. He had stopped at nothing and ended up losing everything in the process.

But he wanted Petra to see the best in him for some reason. Her opinion mattered, and he wasn't entirely sure why.

"Keep the change." He pointed to the tip jar by the register. "I'll be back. I like your shop. I didn't expect

Candlewood Falls to have their own butcher." He figured he'd be forced to buy prewrapped meat from the grocery store, which was okay for just him. But sometimes, like today, he wanted a fresh cut of meat straight from a local butcher. Today, he needed to remember why he loved cooking so much.

Vinny raised a bushy brow. He had more hair in his eyebrows than on his head. He was a short guy with a stocky build. Maybe a wrestler in his youth. His bottom lip fell away when he smiled, revealing a couple of crooked teeth in front.

"My father moved out here in nineteen sixty-nine for cleaner air than what we were breathing in Staten Island. He had terrible asthma."

"Was he a butcher too?"

Vinny pointed to the black-and-white framed picture hanging on the wall behind him. A young man with dark hair, cut close and parted on the side, looked down at a little boy on his knee. The man wore a white t-shirt and an apron not much different than Vinny's. Probably the same one, if he had to guess. The man smiled at the boy who appeared to be putting his tiny fist in the man's mouth.

"That's Dad and me. I was about two. I think. My mom would bring me into the shop. Dad was always working."

"He must've been proud that you went into the family business." He couldn't say the same about his own father.

"He wanted me to get an office job. He didn't want me elbow deep in blood like he was, coming home smelling like a cow. But I loved it here. I loved watching him. So, I took over when he retired. The people who live in this town are good people. For the most part, I guess. They support the local shop owners."

"Well, I'll be returning. Thanks." He raised the meat wrapped in white butcher paper.

"I didn't get your name. I like to know my regular customers."

"Mav. I just moved in a couple of weeks ago. I'm... well, I'm teaching at the community college." The words still tasted strange on his tongue. Him—a teacher.

"Nice to meet you, Mav." Vinny didn't seem to recognize him and he was okay with that. Good about it, in fact.

A phone rang somewhere near the back. "I've got to grab that. I'm solo until this afternoon. Excuse me." Vinny ran off toward the ringing phone.

He took a final glance around the store with its red-and-gray-checkered tile floor. Dried meats hung from the ceiling. A metal rack of shelves held items like crackers, small jars of condiments, and some biscotti cookies. Vinny even had a refrigerator case of homemade sauces and pastas. Staten Island had definitely made its way to Candlewood Falls.

A bulletin board hung by the double glass doors. A few business cards and a couple of flyers were pinned to it. The bright-yellow one with a food truck graphic on top caught his attention. He always loved food trucks.

The flyer said a food truck-style competition was taking place right in town and it was being held the same time his summer cooking class ended. There was an email for team registrations. A few of the guidelines were listed too. His class immediately came to mind. He had been racking his brain on how to teach them. The answer was right here. Competing was something he understood. Cooking to win was what he had done best in his day.

He pushed out into the summer heat and headed for his tiny garage apartment. He had plans to use that fancy grill on Clark's patio. He might as well ask the old man to join him for dinner. He had more than enough.

The old voices took up space in his head while he drove. The food truck-style competition was a mistake. He couldn't compete any longer. He had no right to his dreams when Shelby was dead. He needed to stay in his lane and mind his business. He crumpled the flyer.

Another car, the same model and make as his but black, was parked by the garage he lived over. His brother waited for him on the steps to the apartment. Bash hung his head and rested his elbows on his thighs, but turned at the crunching of tires over gravel. He had a duffel and a computer bag by his feet. Bash had arrived sooner than he expected.

He hopped out of the car with his purchase, and the flyer because he kept his car immaculate—the one thing left from his former life—and met Bash halfway. His brother's clothes were wrinkled and his high-end haircut was pointing in the wrong direction as if he'd been ringing his hands through it.

"Hey," Bash said. "I know it's not Friday yet. I had to come right away. Jess decided she wanted the apartment after all. But for fun, she left all my things on the front lawn and changed the locks. Can you believe it? She's the one who found someone else. Why the dramatics?"

"I don't understand women."

"Me either, obviously. When was the last time you got a haircut? You look like shit." Bash shoved his shoulder.

"Seriously?" He didn't want to point out that he was basically thinking the same thing about Bash. But he couldn't resist pushing his hair off his face. He liked it long. It wasn't like he was in a kitchen anymore. He had no problem with shaving every few days either.

"Just saying. Anyway, can I stay?"

"What about your job? Do you really want to commute from out here? I don't even think the train runs on an express schedule."

"I'm going to work virtually for the rest of the summer." Bash had all the answers.

"Where are the rest of your things?"

"In my office. I don't want to answer any questions there either. I pulled the blinds and locked the door. I told my assistant to stay out of my office until I come back."

"That's some plan." He fought to keep the sarcasm at bay.

"Do me a favor? Save the judgment and the I told you so's and any other advice you might have. I just need a drink and a fucking day off." Bash ran his hands through his hair.

"You're going to go bald if you keep tearing at your hair like that." He let the laugh rip right out of him.

"Shut up." Bash punched his shoulder. It stung.

"Okay. Okay. My mouth is shut." He threw up his hands in surrender. The flyer fell from his grip.

"For once. Hey, what's this?" Bash snagged the flyer and unfolded it.

"It's nothing. For a split second I thought about signing my class up to compete."

"You should do it." Bash shoved the flyer at him.

"Why? They can't cook and I'm no teacher." He glanced at it and shoved it in his pocket.

"You don't give yourself enough credit. You were the king once. You could be again. With the right opportunity."

"And you think this food truck-style competition is it?" He laughed again and headed up the stairs to the apartment. The heat was still thick even in the late afternoon and the bugs were biting his ankles.

"You should enter it. Prove to yourself you still have it. When you win, it will be good for your ego." Bash turned in a circle in the living room. "You can walk from one side of this place to the other in two steps. Where do I sleep?"

"The couch. What do you mean *when I win*? Don't you mean if?" He pulled the flyer out of his pocket and put it on the table. He washed his hands, then seasoned the meat with simple salt and pepper and a steak rub he had found for the times he didn't want to make his own.

The first night here he had unpacked his kitchen supplies. His tools were the one other nice thing he took from his old life. He couldn't part with them even when he had tried. He was glad for them now. His grilling tongs were the best for a thinner steak like the flat iron.

"Mav, there isn't a cooking competition you can't win. Don't you want to go back to the work you love? You can't be happy with the way things have been these past years. I could ask around to see if anyone needs a good chef. Just part-time maybe."

"Bash, don't go there. I'm not stepping foot in someone else's kitchen and I sure as hell don't have what it takes to run my own. This class is enough." More than enough for now. He had three students he didn't know what to do with. And Petra who was riling him up in ways he would rather she didn't. The whole ride over to the coffeehouse all he had wanted to do was take her hand and lace his fingers through hers and feel how soft her skin was.

"You're wrong. But I guess you'll need to figure it out on your own." Bash pulled out his laptop and set it up on the coffee table.

"You know how you just asked me not to judge your life? Well, stop judging mine or go find somewhere else to crash."

"Sorry. Actually, I'm not sorry." Bash faced him with his hands on his hips. "You are the person I have admired most in the world. I always looked up to you because you are my big brother and you never allowed anything or anyone to stop you from getting what you wanted. What happened to Shelby was a tragedy. But you didn't cause it. And once you figure that out, you might start living again. I sure as hell wish you would. I don't know who you've become. But I miss my brother. Send him back."

"That's enough." He slammed the counter with his grilling tongs. They vibrated in his hand and cracked the laminate. Great. He would have to pay for that.

Bash glared at him.

He glared back. Neither of them moved.

A knock came to the door. They both turned. He brushed past Bash and pulled open the door to find Clark.

"Everything all right up here? I heard some yelling." Clark looked between the two of them. He sported a navy baseball cap on his bald head and those overalls again.

"Sorry about that. This is my brother Sebastian. He's going to crash for a couple of days if that's alright." He wanted to hang his head for getting caught fighting with Bash.

"Hello," Clark said with a nod. "Stay as long as you like. I don't mind having the company around. And as long as Mav pays the rent and doesn't burn the place down, his life is his business."

"Thank you, sir. And it's nice to meet you. I'm sorry if we disturbed you. My brother and I were having a disagreement. But it's all settled now." Bash stuck out a hand and Clark shook with him.

"I hope so."

"I was hoping to fire up your grill to make dinner. Would you like to join us?" he said.

"Feel free to use the grill, but I have to pass on the invite. Have myself a date." He tugged on his collar.

"That makes one of us," Bash said.

He wondered how Petra liked her steaks and what her favorite vegetable was. Could he get her to smile for him if he made her a special dish? Those were dangerous thoughts, taking him down a road better left alone.

"You two handsome young men don't have women in your lives? Well, then, you must be doing something wrong if a man my age has a better love life than you two."

"Who would date Mav with that hair?" Bash choked out a laugh.

Clark lifted his cap and rubbed his head. "Son, when all you've got is a cue ball above your neck, any hair at all is a win."

"He's got you there," he said and grabbed the steaks for the grill. Petra probably hated his hair. She seemed too wound up to like anything except the boy next door look. And that wasn't him. Never was. Never will be.

"Are you going to cook those things or make love to it?" Bash said. "You're gazing at them like they have two legs and a nice butt."

Heat filled his cheeks. "You are crude."

He tabled any more thoughts of Petra before more than his eyes gave him away.

CHAPTER EIGHT

P etra opened the door to her parents' bedroom and she didn't have a total meltdown. *See? It's not so bad.*

The real motivator had been the call from her father that she had allowed to go to voicemail. He wanted to know her progress, and she had nothing to tell him. She'd been here a week and hadn't packed one single thing. She had better get to work and dropped the empty packing box on the bed.

The room smelled of lilacs, her mother's favorite perfume. The antique-style glass bottle sat on the silver tray right next to the hairbrush that had been given to Ruby by her mother. Mom had never said which one of her children she wanted to have it. Nyx would scoff at such a formal piece. Ember might like it. Or maybe Paige would want something of her grandmother's. The navy-blue velvet box was also in its usual spot on the dresser. But when she opened it, the rosaries were gone. Instead, there was a folded piece of paper. Her trembling fingers removed the note. Leaving notes was such a Ruby thing to do. But that didn't stop the hammering of her heart. Even her breath refused to leave her lungs.

My dearest Petra,

Thank you for taking on the monumental task of finding a place for my things. When your father told me, I wanted to stop you. You shouldn't have to be burdened with that chore so early in your life. But we don't get our say when the clock runs out. So, I took the burden from you. Dad didn't even notice. What man would? You have given too much to others. Take what's yours. Do what I couldn't well enough. I love you from every part of eternity. Mom.

A spot of ink blurred and spread on the page. When the second tear plopped on the page, she folded the note and returned it to the box before her crying ruined everything.

She pulled open the drawers. They were empty. She ran to the closet. The vacant hangers swung in the breeze the door created. On the top shelf were three brown photo boxes. Each one was printed with the names of Ruby's children. She reached for hers, but stopped. She couldn't handle any more notes tonight. She would call her sisters and tell them what she had found. They could come and get theirs if they wanted. Or not.

She couldn't pack up the few personal items left here. She'd start in the basement. Or maybe the kitchen. She felt safest in the kitchen. But she would not spend another second in this room with her mother's ghost. She hurried from the room, grabbing the velvet box on her way out.

"Mom, what are you doing out here?" Paige stood on the back steps in her sweat shorts and t-shirt. She had piled her hair on top of her head. The light from inside the house painted her in a silhouette.

"I didn't know you were home." She pushed up in the patio chair she had brought out to the lawn. It was darker on the grass and she had wanted to be swallowed up, wrapped in some kind of protection after finding her mother's note. "Did you have fun with your friends?"

"Yeah. Why are you sitting outside?"

"It was too hot in the house. I thought there might be a breeze tonight." She scratched at her ankle where a few mosquitos had made dessert out of her. There was no breeze, and it was just as hot outside as in, but she couldn't stay in the house. The walls had closed in on her. Her mother was everywhere and nowhere at the same time.

Paige grabbed a chair and sat beside her. She must have something she wanted to share. Maybe a replay of the night's events, but Petra wanted a little more alone time. She wasn't sure she had the energy to be the on-call mom at the moment. She was grateful for the dark once again. Her face would be hidden and Paige wouldn't be able to read her thoughts playing out in her expressions.

"What's this?" Paige turned the velvet box in her hands.

She had brought it out with her and left it on the arm of the chair. She wasn't sure why she had taken it out here. Maybe the soft material was comforting. The inside smelled like her mother's perfume. She was the worst daughter, wanting to run from her mom in one breath and wanting her comfort in the next. Had she given her mother enough comfort in the end? She couldn't remember.

"That was Grandma's," she said.

"You finally started packing her things?"

"Actually, Grandma did some of the packing herself." It was just like her mother to take care of her and her sisters no matter how she was feeling. She had always protected her, Ember, and Nyx. It wasn't until she became a mother herself that she realized how much she wanted to keep her child safe. And how impossible a task that was. But her mom had managed, even with a husband like Huck Wilde.

"What's inside?" Paige flipped open the lid. Her face fell. "It's empty."

She simply shrugged. She had put the letter in her planner. It wasn't as if she didn't want Paige to see it. She just wasn't ready to talk about any of it yet. Maybe tomorrow. Maybe next year. Maybe after she had the courage to look inside the photo box with her name on it. Some of her mother's words rang in her ears. Mom wanted her to find a life of her own. She had one once. But life hadn't turned out the way she had scripted it. And her mother knew that. Not from the things Petra had shared with her, but from the things she hadn't. Ruby was always watching her girls from the sidelines and always seemed to know what they needed even when they scoffed at her intrusions.

She fought a groan. Just like her and Paige. Were mothers and daughters everywhere destined to this unachievable dance of love and acceptance?

"Do you want it?" she said.

"The box? Sure, I guess. Will there be any other things

I can keep? I always loved her scarves. She would let me play with them when I was little." A wistful smile crossed Paige's face.

She hoped her mother had remembered how much Paige enjoyed making scarves into magic capes and left a few somewhere in the house. "If we find any, they are yours."

"Thanks." Paige sank back in the chair, tucking her legs under her. "It's pretty here."

"I had forgotten how many stars you can see from the backyard."

"Junior said from the orchard the stars go for miles. They fill up the whole sky. He's going to take me there at night to see it."

What Raf had told her earlier at the coffee shop about the very popular Junior raced across her mind. She tried not to entertain the worry. She didn't need to overreact. Paige had a good head on her shoulders. But that didn't stop her from wanting to know more.

"What's Junior like?" She hoped her question held a pinch of disinterest. She focused on the mosquito bite, keeping her gaze away from Paige's.

"He's nice. Don't really know yet." The wistfulness was gone. A slight edge had taken its place. Most people wouldn't notice, but a mom would. A mom who had tried to pay attention and not miss the important stuff. But she had anyway. For all her trying, they were still at odds.

"Were you at the orchard tonight?"

Paige narrowed her eyes. "No. I just said Junior wanted to take me there. If he had, I would've told you. I don't lie, Mom."

"I know. I'm sorry." She was always sorry where Paige

was concerned. She should have asked more about Junior's job or what he looked like. "I was just curious."

"We're allowed to be on the orchard, if that's what you're getting at. We work there and Grandpa owns it. Someday I could own the orchard, if I wanted." She unfolded from the chair. Her jaw was set and her back straight.

Petra didn't bother to tell her that Grandpa would not will Paige any part of the orchard. As of now, his portion of the orchard was going to his younger brother Silas. And if Silas was gone before him, then Huck's fifth would go to Brad. Huck wanted the orchard in the family, and only run by the men.

That was why she didn't want to discuss a café with Brad. She could end up doing all the work and getting none of the financial credit. She was done with that kind of arrangement. Frank had seen to that with his mismanagement of their money while she was busy trying to make his dreams come true.

"Don't go to the orchard alone at night with a boy you don't know. It's not safe. And you had better ask Brad if he wants anyone in his fields after dark. Someone could get hurt and he'd be liable. So would Uncle Silas and so would Grandpa."

"Fine. I wouldn't want to upset Grandpa." Paige marched back in the house.

"God forbid, we upset *Grandpa*," she muttered under her breath.

She had grown up in a house where they all tried not to upset Huck. Her mother had made it her mission. It wasn't until Ruby became ill that Huck had finally shown outsiders how much he loved his wife. It had been disarming and a relief at the same time.

She pushed out of the chair and walked across the damp grass in her bare feet. Her phone vibrated in her pocket. She hesitated, unsure if she wanted to talk to anyone. But when the call went to voicemail, it rang again.

Nyx's name and a picture of her making a goofy face while eating an ice cream cone popped up on the screen. She wasn't expecting to hear from her youngest sister tonight.

"Hey, Nyx." She tucked the phone between her ear and shoulder. But that position never worked as well as it did when she was kid and could shove the hard plastic receiver from the white phone that hung on the kitchen wall under her ear.

"Petra…" Nyx's words were interrupted by a cry and a hiccup. She sniffled, then said, "It's done. Mom is gone."

Her knees buckled and she sank into the grass, its dampness seeping through her pants. For all the preparedness for this moment, she wasn't prepared at all because a part of her had hoped her mother would change her mind. She didn't want to imagine a world without her mother in it. Ruby was the person she could call and ask about a recipe. When in reality, it had been her way to need her mother without explanation. Food was how they communicated when all the other options were out of reach. She needed more time. She had more questions.

"But Dad didn't give us the heads-up." She dropped onto her butt. The hell with the wet grass and the mosquitos. Huck had promised to tell them before it happened.

"That bastard said we didn't need one." Nyx blew her nose with a fierce honk.

"He called you?"

"I don't know why, believe me. I figured I'd be the last one he'd call. He probably hit my number by mistake. He was upset. I'll give him that. When Ember had said she'd seen him cry, I almost laughed at her. Dad crying is a joke. But holy shit, he was broken up tonight."

"I'm sorry. I didn't mean to sound like he shouldn't have called you first. It's just that…"

"That it should have been you. I know. And considering you're there making things easier for him when he gets back, it should have been you."

Nyx had read her mind. But she hadn't meant to say it. She hadn't meant to think it even. Nyx had a big life in Nashville. Candlewood Falls had been too small for her. Coming here to pack up Mom would have been too much an ask for Nyx.

"Never mind that. Have you called Ember?"

"She's next. Are you going to be okay? Should I tell Ember to come to you? I could even be on a plane tonight and be in New Jersey before sunrise."

"No, no. I'm okay. Don't come here. That's silly. Unless you really want to, I can call Ember. I can run over if she needs me to."

"If you don't mind. I need to pull myself together and get to practice. We're rehearsing for the shows we're doing this fall. I don't want to miss it. God, that sounds so selfish, doesn't it? My mom just passed away and all I can think about is rehearsal. I'm the worst."

"No, you're not. You know who you are. Take care of yourself the best way for you. I'll call Ember. I'll take care of it." She envied Nyx and her complete life. Nyx had always known who she was and went for it, ignoring all the arguing from their parents. Ruby and Huck had wanted her to be practical. Have a backup plan, but Nyx wouldn't hear of it. That was what her mother was trying to tell her in the note. She needed a life of her own too. She wasn't sure how she felt about any of that just now. She'd deal with it later.

"Thanks, Petra. I love that you take care of all of us. I'll be in touch." Nyx ended the call.

She stared at the phone a second. She did take care of everyone else. She put everyone else's needs above her own. And still she pulled up Ember's number.

"Hey," Ember said in her cheery voice.

"I'm coming to your house in five minutes. We're going out." She hung up before Ember could say another word. When Ember called her right back, she texted it was important. She would tell Paige and then go get Ember. After all that, she would have herself a big fat drink.

She sure as hell had earned it.

CHAPTER NINE

Mav could not believe he let Bash talk him into going out. It was almost ten and he had to be up early for class the next day. He had wanted a good night's sleep to be ready to face his small class.

He had spent a few hours after dinner preparing how the class would handle the competition. Maybe he could pull it off. Just this once, he could try and take the lead again.

He thought they were going to Murphy's, the bar in town, but Bash searched on the internet for the best spots and a new brewery had popped up.

Bash pulled into the brewery's parking lot. "Whoa. Did you see that mural?"

"How can you miss it? It's the entire side of this building. Do you know who that guy is?" A picture of a hockey player with a trophy in one hand covered the side of the building. The artwork was fantastic, and he was pretty sure he'd seen that signature somewhere else. Maybe at an exhibit in a museum.

"I have no idea who that is. I think I've only seen one professional hockey game in my life."

"Yeah, me too. Baseball is more my thing. Okay, let's check this place out." Bash pushed out of his car and they went inside.

The place was crowded for a weeknight. The pool tables were occupied with groups of people pushing, laughing, and drinking. The bar was in the center of the room that looked up to the open second floor. The cackle of voices rose in the wide space and bounced off the walls. There was even a stage for a band to play. Industrial but minimal.

"Cool place," he said, wondering what kind of a menu they offered. If it were him, he'd have bites to go with the brews. Definitely a twist on beer battered pretzels. Maybe a burger or chicken sandwich option for those who needed to absorb some of the alcohol.

"Bar?" Bash said and walked away before he could agree.

They grabbed two seats that faced the steel and wood staircase. A few round tops flanked the side of the staircase. His breath caught. Petra and another woman with similar features sat at one of those round high-tops, leaning in toward each other, busy in conversation. Two empty wineglasses and some appetizer-style foods were on the table.

"What are you staring out?" Bash said.

"Huh? Oh, I think that's one of my students." He tilted his chin in Petra's direction.

"Man, you are the luckiest. Only you would get a hot student." Bash laughed and called for the bartender.

"Shut up, will you?" He grabbed the menu to keep

himself busy and act as if the comment didn't fluster him at all. Petra was beautiful and he didn't much like his brother noticing.

"Do you want to go over and say hello?" Bash hit him with his elbow.

"Why would I want to do that?" He ordered a micro-brew. Petra had made it clear earlier that she wasn't up for conversation with him. He would respect their teacher-student relationship. He wasn't looking for friends anyway.

"Because the last time I saw you look at someone that way was when you met Shelby."

He opened his mouth to say that wasn't true, there had been other women who had caught his attention, but nothing came out.

Bash shrugged. "Just saying, man. You deserve a little happiness. The past is the past."

"What is that supposed to mean?" He could never pay the price for what he had done. It would take two lifetimes.

"Forget it. It doesn't mean anything. I don't want to fight with you again. If you don't want to say hello to the lady, then don't. Okay?"

He had survived by not talking about Shelby's accident. In the beginning, he had to tell himself to breathe because thinking about it and answering the constant *are you okay* questions seized his lungs. He had prayed at night for the vengeful god above to take him too because he didn't want to live with what he had done. But he woke up each and every day to live in his own hell.

Bash said something, but he missed it. The noise in the bar crashed against his head like metal lids from cast iron pots. His vision blurred and his heart pounded so hard it hurt. He never should have come here. He never should have let Bash bring up Shelby again.

"Mav?" A female voice came to him down a long tunnel.

He turned toward the sound, but his head moved as if it were in mud. A cool hand pressed against his arm. A beautiful woman smiled at him.

"Petra?" The word tumbled over his lips, but the voice belonged to someone else. He cleared his throat, hoping to jump-start it.

"I thought that was you. I wanted to say thanks again for the ride today."

The room started to fill in behind her. The blurred edges of his vision sharpened, bringing the staircase and the other customers into focus.

"It was no problem. This town is so small that nothing is out of the way."

"Are you okay? You look a little piqued." Her hand remained on his arm and concern flashed over her eyes and framed the edges of her mouth.

"It's really warm in here, don't you think? Were you able to pick up your car?" He could offer her a ride over to the college right now. He didn't want to stay in the brewery any longer. The crowd was too large and noisy. The beer was watery. His brother wasn't the best company. Or maybe that was him. He had stopped being good company a long time ago.

"I found my keys." The concern on her face was washed away with delight. A warmth ran through him. She should smile like that more often. When she did, the blue in her eyes brightened like a summer midday sky.

Bash pushed him from the side.

"Oh." He shot Bash a look, then turned back to Petra. "This is my brother, Sebastian. Sebastian, this is Petra. She is one of my students." He made the introduction that way because he didn't want Petra knowing that he and Bash were discussing her only a few minutes before she walked over.

"It's nice to meet you." Bash leaned over him and stuck out his hand. "What do you think of the class so far? My big brother is the best teacher there is."

He wanted to shove Bash off his bar stool.

Petra gave a quick shake. "We've only had one class. But I'm looking forward to learning a lot."

"I bet." Bash raised his eyebrows.

He slid off the stool and stood with his back to Bash. Laughter bellowed from the pool table area, giving him the excuse to lean in and speak in Petra's ear. "I'm sorry if he was rude. He doesn't know when to keep his mouth shut."

"Family trait?" she teased.

"Excuse me?"

"Never mind." She waved the words away. "I hope you don't mind I came over. I saw you here and the color drain from your face like you saw a ghost or something. I just wanted to make sure you weren't sick." She leaned in closer, and he grabbed a whiff of her sweet scent. He wanted to run his tongue over her neck and see if she tasted as good as she smelled. "Like maybe we shouldn't have eaten here."

"I'm sorry, what did you say?" His last thought had blown out the sound of her speaking.

"Is the food bad here?"

"Oh, no. At least I don't think so. This place got pretty good reviews. You've never been here before?"

"Nope. It's new. That's why we came. Ember wanted me to try it out."

"I don't understand. I thought you were a local."

"I was once. Now I've returned. I'd better let you get back to your brother. He's shooting daggers this way. I'll see you tomorrow." She placed her hand on his arm again and gave a gentle squeeze. The heat from her hand ran up his arm and into his chest.

"I'm looking forward to it." More than she knew, and more than he should say.

"Me too." She flashed him that unbelievable smile and returned to her sister.

He slid back on the stool.

"Yowzah," Bash said, laughing.

"Shut up," was all he could manage.

CHAPTER TEN

Petra stole a quick glance at Mav as she navigated her way back to Ember, downing the last of her drink. The color had returned to his face. When she had spotted him sitting at the bar, he had appeared distraught. It seemed he and his brother were arguing. She had wanted to help him and found her legs had been moving before she could stop herself. But in the end, he was fine. She had probably imagined the pain on his face. It was easier to focus on someone else's needs than her own. She didn't want to think about the pain of losing her mother anymore this evening.

"What did he say?" Ember sucked the olives off the pick. She was going to have to carry Ember home later if she kept mixing martinis and wine.

"Not much." But she had enjoyed the teasing. He could make her laugh. She couldn't remember the last time a man could do that for her. "He's just hanging out with his brother."

"The brother's cute." Ember ran her tongue around the inside of the glass.

"I guess." Mav was far more handsome in that mysterious way than the brother in his high-end polo shirt and that very expensive watch on his tanned wrist. She preferred Mav's shaggy and rugged look. He used to be cleaner cut in his famous days—she had searched the internet for images—but this new look made her skin tingle. She had never been with a bad-boy kind of guy.

"Are you okay?" she said, taking the empty glass away from Ember.

"I think so. It's not like we didn't know this was coming. I just can't believe it's happened. And without any warning." Ember held her chin in her hands.

"We had warning. Six months ago. I kept hoping Mom would change her mind." But she never had. Not even when Petra had mentioned that Mom could go years before she was too far gone. But her mother hadn't wanted to wait until she couldn't decide any longer. Mom had admitted that she would love more time, but time wasn't guaranteed. The only thing that was certain was the end. And Mom wanted to decide when that was.

"She's never been so determined to do anything as much." Ember reached for the glass, but she pulled it away.

"You've had enough."

"I'm dealing with my grief." Ember pouted.

"Find a more suitable way, please."

"Like going home and making love to Raf?"

"Gross, Ember. I don't want to hear about that." She closed her eyes against the visual popping up in her mind.

"You could see if your hottie teacher is game for a

romp in the sheets." Ember tossed her head back and cackled.

"You're drunk." And slightly unlikable at the moment. But if she were being honest, she might like to see Mav with the sheets wrapped around him.

"Yup. But you like him. I saw the way you looked at him, all doe-eyed. Who would've thunk it?" Ember laughed again. "Petra has a crush." Ember wobbled in her seat. "Take me home, sis. I'm missing my man."

Movement caught the corner of her eye. Mav gave her a small wave as he and his brother left the bar. She waved back.

Ember stumbled off the stool. She lunged to catch her before she hit the floor. "Good sex will give you an outlet when you've had enough packing."

"Since I'm way behind on that project, that's how I should be spending all my time. Except for class and whatever homework we get." And not spending time taking care of her very drunk sister.

"Your homework should be him." She pointed in the direction Mav went.

"Please stop it. I don't do flings." She gripped Ember by the elbow and led her toward the door.

"Maybe it's about time you started." Ember burped and slumped in her arms.

"Well, shit."

Petra was the first one in class. The room smelled stale. She threw open a few windows and the rare summer breeze flew in and brushed her hair away from her face.

She stood there for a moment and let it wash over her. Today was a new day. The first full day without her mother in it. Her heart ached and shamefully she felt relief too. The wait was over. There would be no more suffering. Her mother's words in her note echoed in her mind. Get a life. Ember telling her last night to change the way she was caught up in the tangles of her thoughts too. Even if she did take a risk she had never taken before, where would she even begin to find this new life?

"Good morning." Mav's voice startled her away from the window. He looked dashing in his black polo and gray shorts. She wanted a closer look at his tattoos, but she didn't want him to catch her staring.

"Hello." She rubbed her hands over the bottom of her shirt, wishing she had something else to do with them.

"Did you have fun last night?" His salt-and-pepper goatee around that smile disarmed her. The room was too hot again.

"I suppose so." She wasn't going to explain what she and Ember were actually doing. When she had arrived at Ember's, Ember seemed to know before she had even spoke. They had held each other in the doorway of her home and cried. Then they had called Nyx and cried again. After the tears were dried, they had started the seedling of a plan for a memorial service. It had been Raf that had suggested they go to the brewery for a little downtime. He had even offered to drive them, but she had been more than willing to be the designated driver. Getting plastered wasn't something she had wanted to do even if Ember had.

"That's nice. I can't say the same exactly. My brother is a bit pushy sometimes."

"Oh. I'm sorry to hear that." So she wasn't too far off when she had believed that something was wrong last night. He was keeping his problems close to his chest—the way she did. They might have more in common than just enjoying food.

"Don't be. As soon as the others get here, we'll jump right in." He looked out the door in both directions, effectively ending the topic of bumping into each other last night.

"What will we be learning today?" She had wondered about the direction of class this morning in the shower and during her short breakfast with Paige before she ran off to work.

Paige hadn't wanted to discuss her grandmother much more than to say she was glad she wasn't sick anymore. Everyone could agree on that much. She had given Paige some space, allowing her time to deal with her thoughts and emotions. She never knew how much space and how much time was correct. And she always seemed to get it wrong.

"I have a surprise," Mav said, interrupting her thoughts. "You're going to love it." His cheeks were full of healthy color. Almost like an apple's bright red.

Somehow, she wondered how much she would enjoy this supposed surprise, since surprises weren't exactly her thing.

Titi and Niko entered the room before she could vocalize her objections to surprises in general. Mav stepped out of their way. They were deep in conversation about a cooking show they had seen and barely noticed him standing there.

"Great. We're all here," Mav said, rubbing his hands together. "I have an announcement to make."

"When do we being cooking?" Niko jumped in and cut Mav off. Niko took the same seat he had occupied before. He wore a blue-checked short-sleeve button-down shirt and crisp jeans. His hair was combed neatly in place and smoothed with some kind of pomade.

"Sooner than you think." Mav's gray eyes sparkled like a sun-filled lake.

Titi opened the double-door refrigerator in the back. Her rings caught the overhead lights and cast a rainbow of colors around the room. Her faded navy-blue dress hung in a straight line, pooling over the top of her feet. "There aren't any fresh ingredients in here."

"No. No. Not yet." Mav shoved his thumbs into his front pockets, his shoulders slouched. The gesture reminded her of Paige when she was younger and trying to win over an argument to stay up later. She covered her mouth to hide her smile.

"I'll have a fully stocked kitchen soon. I wanted to explain something today before we begin. And go over some basics."

"I thought we'd be cooking every day." Titi's voice whined like a violin out of tune.

"We will be. We'll be practicing every day. Starting tomorrow. Titi, have a seat so I can tell you what I have planned for the next four weeks." Mav pointed to an empty seat in the front row.

Titi plopped into her chair and dumped her bright-pink handbag on the floor beside Niko's feet.

"I signed the class up for a food truck-style competition." Mav's face beamed with delight. She half expected him to slap his thigh and have a hearty laugh.

"What does that mean?" she said. There hadn't been any mention of competitions in the class description. She wasn't a good enough cook to win any contests. She doubted her two other classmates were either. If this was some plan to set them up for failure, she would march right into the admissions office and let them know how poorly run this class actually was. She didn't care that he was charming and even a little sweet and that last night when he had such a pained expression on his face that she wanted to make that pain go away. She came to this class to move the needle of her life a little. She needed to accomplish something for herself.

"It means that instead of me coming up with new recipes every couple of days and you never having the time to really get one right, we only have to come up with three and perfect them. If we win, then you'll all get As for the class."

"I don't want to compete," Niko said.

"Why not? It will be fun." Titi would be the one to suggest the joy in this idea. That woman seemed to float on positivity.

"It's not much different than if I gave you a final exam. This way you can all work together as a team. Which is how a real kitchen works anyway."

"If one person on the team screws up, then the whole team fails," Niko said, shooting her a dubious glare.

"Why are you looking at me? You're the one whose wife signed you up for this class. At least I came here of my own volition." She hadn't meant to snap, but the words had flown out of her mouth. She was tired, that was all. It had been a late night, and now this idea of a competition set her on edge.

"My wife may have registered me, but I used to be a cook in the Army. I'm not bad. Not as good as our fearless teacher here." Niko pointed at Mav. "I searched you. You've won more awards than any other chef your age."

At least Mav had the decency to look embarrassed. "My past is not in play here, and I want it kept that way." A darkness passed over his eyes. She shivered even in the warm classroom.

"I'm not doing a competition with two women who can't cook." Niko stood. "My final grade isn't going to depend on someone else."

"Why do you care so much about your grade? We're not getting a degree here. This is just for fun." Titi swung her hand in the air.

"Taking pride in your work matters," Niko said.

"Wait one second." Titi popped up out of her chair too. "Don't you go accusing us of not taking pride in our work. You haven't even seen us in action. It's day two. Are you afraid two women might be better than you?"

Niko blanched. "I didn't say that."

"Sounds to me like you did." She crossed her arms over her chest. She liked Titi and her outspoken personality.

Titi stood beside her, placing a hand on her shoulder. "Sorry, Niko, but you sounded exactly like a chauvinist who thinks he's better than a woman."

"Aren't you going to jump in here?" Niko looked at Mav.

"Looks to me like you're digging your hole just fine by yourself." Mav smirked. She wanted to stay mad at him too. But that little smile and the affirmation on their behalf melted some of the uncertainty around her heart.

"What happens if we lose the competition?" Niko said.

"Unfortunately, you'll all get a failing grade too. I'm sorry about that. I checked with the department yesterday. I can do this, but it's basically a pass or fail system that way."

"I know the grade shouldn't matter," Niko said. "We aren't matriculating, but I've never failed a class before. I don't really want to start now. It doesn't sit right with me."

"Come on, Niko. Who says we're going to fail? We have Mr. Labraccio here as our teacher. You just said he's award-winning. We can do it." Titi fist-pumped the air. "Don't be such a chicken."

"Petra, what about you? You haven't said much." Mav held her gaze. "Are you in?"

She had no idea if the three of them, plus Mav could win any cooking competition. She stole glances at her classmates. Titi gave her an encouraging nod. Niko shrugged. The decision was coming down to her.

She might not be a professional cook, but she had been making meals for her family for twenty years. Her friends always raved about her cooking. They could pull this together if they tried. But there was something she needed to know first. "Why don't you want to teach us the way the coarse description stated?"

He dropped into the chair behind the teacher's desk. "I thought the competition would be more fun than a regular class."

She held his gaze. "Is that the truth?"

"Why wouldn't it be?" The air between them charged. Nobody moved.

"I'm just wondering why you would change the plan at the last minute. You're putting a lot of pressure on us, and we didn't have a say in it."

Mav stood up. "I don't know what any of you expected from this class. But when I'm running a kitchen, I do it my way. Busy kitchens are nothing but pressure. And if you can't keep up or stand the heat as they say..." His words fell away. "We're doing the competition. If you don't like it, drop the class. There's still time to get your money back. If you're not afraid to compete, I'll see you tomorrow." He marched out of the class without another look back. The door closed with a whoosh.

"Well, that's just great," Niko said.

"Stop all your complaining." Titi shook her head. "I say we do it. And I'm going to ask the both of you to at least give it a try. If either one of you drops, the whole class will be canceled. At least finish out the week. Maybe then, if you go, I can convince the school to keep the class going."

"Are you going to compete in the food truck competition by yourself?" Niko smirked.

"No, but then maybe I can convince Mr. Labraccio to teach me how to boil water. Please. I don't have anything else going on in my life at the moment. I don't want to lose this too."

She didn't have anything else in her life either. She didn't want to fail so publicly and embarrass herself. Ember had made a real go of her bakery business and was doing a great job. Nyx was a superstar. Even their father had the well-run, family-owned orchard. She had failed at helping Frank with his business. She had failed at being a mother. And if she didn't finish packing before her father returned, she would have failed that too.

Titi and Niko stared at her as if waiting for her answer.

Something stirred inside her. Probably fear. But after the year she had had, she needed something that was hers. What if they actually won? What if she could prove to herself she could do it? For once.

"Petra, what do you say? Us girls need to stick together," Titi said.

"Okay. I'm on board." This ridiculous competition would give her something to fight for.

"Excellent. Niko?"

Niko shook his head. "Fine. I'll stay. But don't say I didn't warn you. The other teams are going to mop the floor with us. I'll see you both tomorrow." He went out the door.

"Thank you," Titi said.

"There's no need for thanks." She gathered her bag.

"You need this too, don't you?"

"Maybe. I don't know." She searched inside her tote just to avoid Titi's stare.

"I do. I can see it in your eyes."

Clearly, she hadn't hid her truth well enough.

CHAPTER ELEVEN

Mav knocked on Clark's back door. He hadn't seen the man all day. The temperatures had climbed well into the nineties, and the sticky humidity made a stroll difficult. Maybe Clark had decided to stay inside where it was cool.

He had made roasted asparagus with goat cheese and mini-turkey meat loaves for dinner. As usual, he had made too much for him and Bash. He thought Clark might like some. The meat loaves were better the next day, anyway, making great leftovers.

"Comin,'" Clark called out from inside the house. He opened the door in his loose overalls and white t-shirt. A gleam of sweat covered the top of his bald head. His cheeks were bright red.

"Are you okay?" Probably not the first thing he should've said.

"Of course, I'm okay. Why wouldn't I be?" Clark narrowed his eyes.

"You look…" He had always hated it when other

people fussed over him after the incident. Clark was probably a lot like that. "Never mind. I had extra. Wasn't sure if you had dinner yet." He handed over the plate wrapped in tinfoil.

"Come inside. The kitchen is in shambles so don't mind the mess." Clark led him through a small mud room with a washer and dryer, cabinets above the appliances, and a bench with several pairs of tattered and worn shoes under it.

The mud room opened up into the kitchen. Well, what was supposed to be the kitchen. Half the cabinets had been torn down. The floor was pulled up, revealing the subfloor. The refrigerator was away from the wall, but still plugged in. A piece of plywood covered the spot where the sink should be.

"You doing a reno?" The only chair in the room was one of those old-style metal and vinyl chairs that doubled as a step stool. His grandmother used to have one in her kitchen.

"You're a bright one." Clark put the dish on the only empty spot on the counter. He had tools spread out across their surfaces.

"Are you doing it by yourself?" He couldn't imagine this older man taking on the task of demolition and then rebuilding an entire kitchen. That was a lot of work for a man half Clark's age.

"Do you see anyone else here?" Clark's ornery tone snapped against his skin like a rolled-up dish towel being flicked against his leg.

"How's the project going?" From the looks of it, pretty bad, but he would let Clark tell the story if he wanted. And if he didn't, then he would mind his own business.

He had enough problems with his cooking class not wanting to do the competition and his brother sharing that small apartment with him.

"Ah, slow. The work takes me longer than it used to. I got this harebrained idea to update a few things in here. You know, in case I decide to sell and move to Florida like every other New Jerseyan. But one thing led to another and now this." Clark waved his hand through the air.

"How are you eating?"

"Microwave still works. Plugged her in in the dining room. And I've got one burner on the stove that operates with a jiggle. I can boil some water. What else do I need? Not like I'm entertaining anyone these days."

"Let me help you." The words were out of his mouth like lightning. And there wasn't a damn thing he could do to grab them and shove them back.

"You?" Clark laughed. "No offense."

The comment and the laugh stung. He was good with his hands and not just in the kitchen. He had installed the kitchen in his restaurant. He had remodeled the kitchen in the house he shared with Shelby. He knew the difference between a two-by-four and a measuring cup.

"Why not me?"

"Aren't you a teacher?"

"What does that have to do with anything?" He wasn't much of a teacher. He couldn't believe his students were against his competition idea. A little healthy competition was good for the soul. It would force them to work hard. Harder than if he showed up with a few recipes and told them to cook. Where was the fun if there wasn't anything at risk? He had hoped Petra would champion for him, but she had wavered. That hurt the most.

"Nothing, I guess. You don't strike me as the building type, that's all." Clark moved the dish to the fridge. "For lunch tomorrow. Thanks for bringing by the food."

"You're welcome. If you decide you need an extra pair of hands, let me know." He would go back to his apartment and watch television or something. Being new in town meant he didn't have any friends here. Other than Bash, he didn't have anyone to grab a beer with.

"Mav…"

He turned.

"If you're offering and all." Clark shrugged. "I wouldn't want to insult you. But it's not like I need you. 'Cause I don't."

"Of course not. The thought never crossed my mind. Afternoons good? I can come by after my class." He hadn't meant to insult the man. He understood pride way better than most. When he had lost his restaurant because he had been too busy drinking his problems away, his pride had hurt so badly he couldn't breathe. All his problems had been his own doing.

"I like the sound of that. See you then." Clark gave a small wave. A quick smile twitched the old man's lips. He almost didn't see it.

"See ya." He let himself out. Gray clouds had rolled in and the wind had picked up. The eerie twinkle of wind-chimes played in the distance. The air smelled like freshly cut grass and rain. A summer storm was on its way in.

He used to love to sit on his porch in his old house and watch as the rain fell and the wind shoved the trees to the side. The thunder would shake him to his core. He didn't have a porch here. He wondered what Petra thought of thunderstorms and then berated himself for the thought. Still, he couldn't stop himself from imagining the wind sweeping her hair away from her face or what she might look like wrapped in one of his sweatshirts as the temperatures dropped.

The rain was only a drizzle. He sat at the top of the stairs to his apartment. The small overhang gave him some coverage. Bash was out for the night, not expected back until tomorrow. Bash had friends. Bash had a job he loved.

He dug out his phone and pulled up an email from Avery with the class list attached. He knew he shouldn't do this. Wasn't allowed. Could probably get himself and Avery in a lot of trouble. But that didn't stop him. When did he ever really stop when he wanted something? Wasn't that how his whole life blew up? Well, now he had nothing to lose. He'd already lost it all.

He pulled up the students' information. There was Petra's name, address, and phone number. There was also an email address. But he didn't want to send an email. It would be too late by then. No, he wanted to watch the storm with her. She had intrigued him, and he wanted to know a little more. Just a little. Nothing too much. Nothing that would end up hurting either one of them.

He punched in her phone number and waited while it rang.

Petra ran downstairs. The wind had made the house creak and the storm clouds turned afternoon to night in a split second. Turning on the lamps did nothing to ease her nerves. She hated storms. It was a foolish childhood fear that she had never outgrown. Nyx and Ember would always tease her. Even Frank had had his fun with her when a storm would roll in and shake the house at its core.

She had wished Paige were home. But she and Paige had gone to blows right before dinner. Petra didn't want her driving around tonight with the storm predicted, but Paige would have none of it. She insisted that if she left right away, she would get to Junior's before the storm and they would stay at his place until after. She had suggested Paige invite Junior to their house, but Paige didn't want that either. Before she knew it, voices were elevated—mostly Paige's—and Paige left. But her child must've felt some guilt because she had received a text when Paige had arrived at her destination. She hoped Raf was wrong about Junior, but that didn't stop her mother's instincts from reaching high alert. Paige could get hurt if she wasn't careful. Hearts were like glass.

She pulled baking dishes out of the bottom cabinet by the stove. Her mother had several stacked like a precarious Jenga game. Some dishes were made of glass, ironically. Some stoneware. A few metal ones she had used for baking were pushed to the back. Petra would give the newer-looking metal ones to Ember.

She ran a hand across the glass dish that had a chip in the corner. How many meals had her mother made in this? Probably hundreds. Tears filled her eyes. It was only a glass dish and it had the power to transport her to a Sunday afternoon when her mother showed her how to make lasagna. She loved those times with Ruby when it was just the two of them. She didn't have to share her mother with her sisters or her father. Ruby was all hers and she could sneak up and wrap her arms around her mom's waist and steal a hug. She could use a hug from her mother now. She needed her mother to tell her she wasn't doing a bad job with Paige. Or hadn't done a bad job and that the future wouldn't include one sans Paige.

Her phone vibrated against the counter, making her jump. "Get it together," she said to herself.

She didn't recognize the number on the screen. She was tempted to let it go to voicemail, but the first rumbles of thunder were in the distance and even talking to a telemarketer for a minute was better than being completely alone.

"Hello?" She grabbed the pots from the next cabinet.

"Hi. Is this Petra?" A male voice, deep with a hint of a gravel came across the line.

She stood, not expecting to hear a man on the other end. She had been hoping for a female solicitor who was selling insurance, at home in her kitchen trying to make ends meet.

"Who's calling?" She wasn't going to give herself away before she knew who was on the other end.

"This is her teacher from the cooking class. Is she available?"

Mav was calling her? She searched the room as if he were standing right there and not on the phone. Or as if he would bolt out from behind the wall. She was losing her mind. But she did like the way his voice made her belly warm.

"Hi, Mav. How can I help you?" Maybe he needed a recommendation for a dinner place or a doctor or something neighborly like that.

"This is going to sound crazy, but I was wondering if you were free?"

"Now?" Her voice took off like a shot. She couldn't see him now. She was in the middle of tearing apart the kitchen. The air conditioning didn't quite reach into here and she had started sweating just from bringing in the packing boxes.

He choked out a laugh. "Yeah. Are you free?"

"To do what?" She must sound like a priggish nun. But she couldn't imagine what Mav would want with her.

"I wanted to watch the thunderstorm. I thought maybe you could watch it with me," he said as if that were a simple request he had made of her often.

"Who watches a thunderstorm?" She slapped a hand over mouth to quiet the obnoxious woman who kept showing up.

But he laughed again. "Me. I love to. Watching it at the beach is best, but we don't have time to drive down to the shore. How about if we sit on my apartment steps unless you happen to have a porch. Porches are good."

Well, she had a wonderful porch, but not for that. Didn't he know how dangerous a storm could be? She had done significant research on the internet about it. She had recently watched a video where a man was standing on his porch and got struck by lightning. The force threw him twenty feet.

"I'm sorry. I don't watch storms." As if to make a point, the rumble of thunder grew louder. She gripped the counter and held her breath. She would have to get off the phone. She thought she had read somewhere it was dangerous to be on the phone in a storm. She would need to check that.

"You have something against storms?"

"Well, kind of. They're dangerous. You shouldn't be outside watching them. You should be locked up nice and tight in a basement." Which is where she would go if the storm was bad.

"I promise we won't sit under any trees and if it gets too nasty, we can move inside."

"I don't understand, Mav. Why is watching a storm so important? And why are you calling me? Don't you have anyone else to watch the storm with?"

"I called you because you're the only other person I know in town besides my brother who isn't here right now. I didn't want to spend the whole night alone. I don't know about you, but long stretches of time without something to do in them sometimes cause me trouble. Empty nights aren't always my friend."

She could relate. She went into the small room her mom used for reading and dropped into the soft chair. Books filled the shelves from floor to ceiling, muffling the thunder. "Right after I got divorced, I would pace my house for hours trying to fill the time and the quiet. It was weird and wonderful at the same time." She didn't know why she just said that. Maybe it was all the emotions of the day coming to a head or the fact fatigue weighed down on her and she couldn't shake it. "I haven't told another soul that."

"Are you alone now?" His voice was low and soothing.

"Unless you count the packing boxes and the pots and pans on the kitchen counter." The packing could wait. She wanted to keep most of the kitchen stuff anyway. It all reminded her of her mother and she could put the things to good use. Not that she was going to learn anything valuable in this cooking class. But she wouldn't say that. Mav was being nice to her.

"Are you moving?"

"Not exactly."

"Then what exactly?"

"It's a long story. Maybe another time. I can't promise I'll go outside on the porch when the storm really hits, but if you want to come here for a little while I could make us some tea. If you want something stronger, you'll have to bring it. I'm out."

"I'll be right over. And tea is great." He ended the call so fast she couldn't take her invitation back.

She sent Mav her address and then wondered how he had her number. Probably from the class list.

What was she doing inviting her teacher to her house? To her parents' house? What would Paige say if she came home and saw a strange man here? But there was something about his rough edges she wanted to run her fingers over. She had been lonely for so long. A little male company wasn't a crime. She was an adult. And if she were going to listen to her mother's words in that note, it was high time she got on with her life.

But Mav might not be thinking of her as anything other than a friend. He was lonely. He had admitted as much. She couldn't confuse loneliness on either of their parts with something more. And she sure as heck wasn't watching any storm from the porch. The rain shifted and tapped against the window with bony fingers. A chill ran over her.

She had about five minutes before he was there. She ran upstairs and brushed her teeth and washed her face. She swapped her stretched out t-shirt for her old reliable black one. It hid all the imperfections that only she seemed to see.

And just to play it safe, she dialed Ember's number.

"Hey, sis. What's happening?" Ember's buoyant voice danced over the line.

"I'm having company." She blurted it out like a pimple popping.

"That's great. Who is it? That eccentric woman from your class? What was her name again?"

"Titi. It's not her. It's the teacher." She checked out the front window for any sign of Mav's car. The rain blew across the glow of the porch lights, but no sign of Mav yet.

"What?" Ember yelled loud enough that she had to move the phone away from her ear.

"Don't make a big deal out of this. He asked me to hang out. That's all." His request was not a big deal. She was simply doing the man a favor. Tomorrow they would go to class and he'd be ornery again because no one wanted to do his dumb competition.

"That's all, my ass. Hey, Raf," Ember said away from the phone. "Petra has a date."

"It's not a date. Why did I call you?" Was it a date? That was ridiculous. Mav wasn't interested in her. He wanted company, and she was his only choice. If his brother had been home, they would be sitting on his steps dodging the lightning. She wouldn't have been a thought to him. In fact, if she had thought about that when they were on the phone, she would have told him no way. If he wanted to spend time with her like a respectable gentleman, he would have given her some notice.

"You called me because you wanted to share the good

news." Ember's voice brought her back to the front room of the house and the storm swirling around her front yard.

"No, I wanted someone to know I had a visitor in case I end up dead." She didn't really think Mav would harm her. But it couldn't hurt to let someone else know a male visitor was coming over. Only until she got to know him better. She didn't know anything about the real him. She hadn't searched him to the depth Niko and Titi had. She was too busy watching videos about men getting blasted off their porches by lightning.

"Stop watching those crime shows. Wear red. It's a good color on you," Ember said.

"I'm wearing my black t-shirt." She glanced down. The shirt was a little wrinkled and somehow a tiny hole had formed near the hem. She ran upstairs to change. Not because Ember told her to, but because she didn't want Mav to think she didn't care about her appearance. She grabbed another black t-shirt. She had too many of these.

"The low-cut one?"

"No." She hated that Ember knew her wardrobe as well as she did and that Ember knew what her choice would be.

"Go change."

"Stop being so bossy. Nothing is happening, Ember. He just needs a friend." And if she were being honest, so did she. She didn't have a lot of girlfriends. She never seemed to fit in with the other mothers in town who did their children's homework for them and baked a hundred cupcakes for the entire town's recreation soccer teams on a Sunday night at eleven. She was never that put together.

"Something is happening, Petra. You invited a man over. Good for you. It's about time you did something for yourself. And make sure you wear the good bra too. Not the sensible one I know you have on."

"Please stop it." The doorbell rang, sending a shiver of fear down her spine. "He's here. I have to run."

"Don't do anything I wouldn't do." Ember laughed.

"Don't worry. I won't. Love you." She ended the call and ran toward the door, but stopped right before she pulled it open. What was happening here? She didn't have to define it. Ember certainly wouldn't have. Ember would go with the flow and let whatever happened, happen. But she wasn't Ember. She needed some guidelines and wasn't going to get any. He rang the bell a second time.

Answer? Pretend she wasn't home? She shook her head at her silly behavior and answered the door. "Hi."

"Hi." Mav's smile creased the lines around his eyes. He wore a t-shirt and shorts, but the shirt stretched over his biceps, outlining them. He had strong arms that could probably make a woman feel safe wrapped in. She liked the tattoos more and more.

Lightning lit up the sky behind him. She flinched with a screech.

His smile dropped. "You okay?"

"Um... it's... I wasn't expecting the lightning right then. Sorry. Hi. Do you want to come inside?" She hoped for inside, but he shook his head.

"You have an amazing porch. The storm is just getting going. Let's sit outside for a few minutes. I brought some asiago cheese and crackers. Not much, but I thought we could munch a little." He held up a small insulated bag. The deep creases around his eyes returned.

He hadn't smiled much in the classroom. If he had, he would have received a better reception to his competition idea. The softness in his gray eyes made it hard to refuse him. She didn't want to tell him how much the storm scared her. But she wasn't sure she could stay outside either.

"Well, alright. Let's sit on the porch for a few minutes. Before the rain really picks up," she found herself saying as if she were someone who was used to watching bad weather sweep through and cause destruction.

"It's just a small thunderstorm. It will pass quickly." He held out his hand.

She slipped hers into his warm grip. His rough skin scraped against hers. He probably built those callouses on holding his index finger to the knife and run-ins with things like his peeler. She hesitated, wishing she could stand there holding his chef's hand in the safety of her home, but she forced her feet to move. She needed to do this and not be the person who ran when things were overwhelming.

She followed him to the porch, keeping her eyes on the spot between his shoulders. He turned and smiled at her. The grays of his eyes charged, almost like the storm, but safer. He pulled out the snacks and placed them on the small table between the two rocking chairs. Thunder shook the earth and her throat closed up. Eating seemed like an impossible task.

"So, why don't you like storms?" He handed her a cracker with cheese on a napkin.

"I like them." She sat in the rocker, leaving the food on her lap.

He raised a brow. "You could have just said as much on the phone. You didn't have to entertain me." The words were softened with kindness and the smile was back. He dropped into the chair next to her.

"You sounded like you needed company." She couldn't meet his gaze. She was the one who needed the company.

"Ah, the pity invite."

Her head snapped up. "It wasn't out of pity. I'm sorry. I shouldn't have said that." She was going about this all wrong. It didn't matter if she had worn an evening gown with a slit up her thigh instead of her practical t-shirt. She had no idea how to be with a man any longer. She had been with Frank for so many years, she had forgotten the dance of playful banter.

He tilted his head back and laughed. "I was teasing you."

"Oh." The rain pounded as hard as her heart. Some drops splashed off the railing and splattered before her feet.

"I'm sorry. I'm bad at being in other people's company. I'm out of practice. Usually I keep to myself and now I see why. I should have said thank you for inviting me. I really did want the company. And not just anyone. I could have hung out with my landlord, but I was thinking of you." His voice lowered and rumbled in her belly. He was inches away. She noticed a few small holes in his earlobe. Tattoos and piercings. Everything they implied made her quiver.

"Why?" Her own voice was barely audible over the rain.

"You sneak into my thoughts. I'll be thinking about anything else, and then there you are."

Heat flushed her cheeks. "But you don't know me."

"I know enough." He took her hand in his again, rubbing her knuckles with his thumb.

She didn't know what to say to that. *Thank you* seemed like the wrong thing. The silence hung between them thick and uncomfortable like the humidity. She eased her hand away, unsure of the next move.

"If I'm making you uncomfortable, I can go. I'm probably violating some teacher-student ethics thing anyway. I was never good at following the rules." He pushed out of the chair.

A jagged white line cracked open the dark sky. Thunder rolled in fast on the *thwack* of lightning and shook the house. She lurched. The cheese and crackers tumbled to the ground. She hurried into the house, not caring how foolish she looked.

Mav followed her inside and closed the door.

"I can't stay outside. I'm sorry." She wanted him to leave. Her cheeks burned again with the heat of humiliation. She was behaving like a child, but she couldn't stop herself. And she didn't want Mav to see her this way.

"It's okay, really. I didn't mean to force you to do something you're afraid of."

"You didn't force me. I wanted to try."

"May I ask why storms upset you so much?" He leaned against the wall and shoved his hands in his pockets.

She appreciated the space he gave her. "How about some tea. I need something to do with my hands."

"I can go, if you want. Just say it, Petra. Tell me what you want."

The rain pummeled the house and the wind whipped around, making the siding moan from the force. She was up to her neck in humiliation. What was a little more?

"Please stay." She led Mav into the kitchen, forgetting

about the boxes and the half-emptied cabinets until they stopped her in her tracks.

"So, you are moving," he said.

"My mother recently passed away. I'm packing up her things before my dad returns." She had said it, and she didn't fall to pieces.

She busied herself with filling the kettle and grabbing mugs while the storm raged on outside. The lights flickered, but remained on. She breathed a sigh of relief.

"I'm sorry about your mom. I lost my mom too," he said.

"That's terrible. I'm sorry." Her heart ached for them both, but she tried to be grateful for the forty-plus years she had with her mom. Some people weren't that lucky.

"It was a long time ago. You never answered my question about the storm. Were you caught in one as a kid or something?"

"Oh, it's so dumb. I must've been in middle school. My mom wanted to take us to the beach for the day, and she wanted my dad to come too. Three kids all under the age of twelve could be a lot, I guess. I think she just wanted the extra pair of hands." And maybe to enjoy the sand and sun for a few hours without having to worry about which daughter wanted or needed what. She could understand that now as a mother, who had tried to carve off moments of time for herself without having to feel guilty about it.

"But your dad didn't want to come and a storm caught you by surprise on the drive down," he said as if he knew the story.

"You have the part right about my dad not coming. He was too busy with work. That was always his excuse. Still was until my mom got sick recently. Anyway, we made it to the beach. My mom set up chairs and towels and an umbrella. We weren't there more than an hour when the storm rolled in."

She pictured the dark clouds invading from the west, their thick line cutting into the blue sky like a fungus. The wind had grabbed hold of the umbrella and sent it end over end down the beach. Nyx had run after it.

"Did you get stuck on the beach?"

"Under the boardwalk, actually. My mom yelled for my younger sister Nyx to come back and forget the umbrella. Nyx is the youngest of the three of us and the strongest willed. But Nyx couldn't hear our mom over the wind and the crashing waves. So, I chased her, but somehow I lost sight of her and my mom. The rain had fallen like a sheet, making it difficult to see. I had run so far down the beach by the time the storm had plowed in. Everyone was gone. I didn't know where to go so I hid under the boardwalk until a lifeguard found me a few hours later."

She had been soaked through and shivering since the only thing she was wearing was her pink bikini that she had begged her mother to get for her because all the girls at the town pool had one. She had clung to one of the pillars under the boardwalk that drove deep into the sand. She had cried the entire time, her tears mixed with the rain and the salt air.

"What did your mom do?"

"She had locked my sisters in the car and went looking for me in the storm. When she had found me, she was so furious because she was going to have to explain to my father why we were so late." The tea kettle whistled, and she recoiled again. She wouldn't be able to settle down until the storm passed.

"Is there somewhere a little more comfortable we could sit?" Mav eased her aside and poured the water into the mugs. "Why don't you let me do this? Do you take honey?"

She shook her head.

"I would suggest we cook something to take your mind off the storm, but I'm afraid you'll jump with a knife in your hand and cut your fingers off."

"It's okay. The tea is enough. And I appreciate the company." Mav's presence in her kitchen, his broad shoulders and height, gave her a sense of comfort. But it wasn't only his build. His caring and not poking fun at her gave her a space to breathe. Frank would always make her feel worse or embarrassed by her fear.

"A cold snack maybe? I left the crackers and cheese on the porch. They're probably toast by now."

A snicker of a laugh escaped her lips. "You did not just say that."

"Bad pun?" He wrinkled his nose. The light in his eyes twinkled.

"I'd say so." But she was warm for the first time since the rain had begun. He made her feel at ease, something she wasn't used to.

"They can't all be winners. May I?" He pointed at the cabinets, but didn't wait for her reply. He opened and closed doors, including the fridge, until he found hummus and carrots. The carrots were precut because Paige liked to snack on them. In the pantry he found pita bread and warmed it in the toaster over. "I promise I won't run the appliance for more than a minute."

She wasn't worried any longer even though the weather outside wasn't letting up. She grabbed a plate and some napkins and motioned for him to follow her into the den with its bookcase and fireplace.

"It's cozy in here." He took the seat opposite hers and stretched out his long legs.

She tried not to stare, but his defined calf muscles had caught her attention. Her gaze trailed up his leg to the hem of his shorts. For a second, she wondered what was underneath them and almost dropped the mug of hot tea all over herself.

"Careful." He righted the mug before the hot water could scald their skin. His fingers brushed against hers, sending more warm shivers over her.

She had no business falling for her teacher. And not just her teacher, but a man who once was the top chef on the East Coast. He must've had tons of women throwing themselves at him.

"I'm such a klutz. I guess I'm still a little freaked out." More like freaked out that a handsome man was in her house, making her think things she hadn't thought in a very long time.

"Would you like me to light us a fire?"

That would make the room too warm and too much like a date. Which this wasn't. Or shouldn't be. "That's okay. I'm sure the storm will pass soon and you can get back home. I doubt you had planned on spending the night with me in my house, drinking tea."

He put the mug on the table and leaned forward with his arms on his thighs. "Petra, I couldn't think of one thing I would rather have been doing than sitting here with you tonight."

"I'm sure that's not true. But thank you for saying it, just the same." This conversation electrified the air between them.

"You don't like compliments, do you?" He cradled the mug and rested it against his chest. His face was free from worry creases. A small smile tugged at his lips.

"That's ridiculous. Of course, I do. Everybody does." She wasn't used to hearing them, that's all.

"What if I told you that you had the most beautiful blue eyes I've ever seen?"

She bit back the first words that popped into her head. "You're trying to charm me, Mr. Labraccio. You can save it for your fans."

The lightning lit up the sky and the yard outside the window. The trees bent against the force of the wind. A few branches of the old oak tapped against the roof as if the storm wanted in on their conversation.

He barked out a loud laugh. "Maybe I am trying to charm you, as you say. Is there anything wrong with that?"

Thunder snapped loud enough to block out her next thoughts. She pushed out of the chair and paced the room in time to the whirl of the wind.

She hated the thunder almost as much as the lightning. Thunder couldn't do any damage, but the storm could. The storm was upon them now in full force just like it had been that day so long ago at the beach. The earth had trembled under her cold feet back then, and the wood floors shook under her now. She had made a pact with God when she was a child that if he let her mom find her, she would follow all the rules for the rest of her life. She had held up her end of things by doing what was always expected of her. Not rocking the boat. Not expressing her needs. Playing it safe had amounted to almost nothing. It had been a childish plea, one she should have not honored.

Mav came to her and stilled her pacing by placing his hands on her shoulders. The lights flickered again, but this time went out, throwing them into complete darkness. She jumped into Mav's arms and he circled her waist with his strength and pulled her against him. His chest was solid. His breath was warm on her face. She couldn't see his eyes, but that was better. He might be looking at her as if she were a fool, afraid of the dark, needing a man to feel safe with.

His hands cupped the back of her head and his lips pressed against hers. The kiss rocked her straight to her toes the way the storm rocked the house. The howling of the wind faded away as the roar in her head grew. She pressed against him and ran her fingers through his hair. Soft, like she had thought.

He sighed against her mouth. "Was that the storm or was that us?" His voice dropped again and tickled her skin as if a rose petal had brushed against her.

She ran her fingers over his jaw. "Us. I hope. Maybe we should try again to make sure."

So, she kissed him.

CHAPTER TWELVE

H e wanted the kiss to go on forever. She tasted like honey on apples and smelled just as good. But a warning in Mav's mind demanded to be heard. He forced the thoughts of guilt and betrayal away. Shelby had been gone for years now, and he had been alone. There was no crime in kissing another woman.

And still the guilt climbed up his throat and wrapped around his windpipe, choking all the air from him. His head spun and the room tilted. This wasn't just any kiss. He could fall hard for this woman, find a place for her inside his broken heart. And that scared him far more than this storm scared her. He pulled back and cut the kiss off.

"I'm sorry." He couldn't think of another thing to say.

Petra backed away. The room was still dark except for the flashes of lightning outside. The thunder took longer to make its presence known. The storm was rolling out of town, much like the heat between them. He had messed up, kissing her. He had to see this woman in class.

"You don't have to be sorry." Her words were almost a whisper. She had moved farther from him. "I should be. I kissed you that last time."

"We can't do that again."

Petra gasped.

His mind circled through too many thoughts from the moment she was in his arms against his chest, to the way his head nearly exploded when her tongue met his, and the way his body responded to her. And yet, with each thought, he settled back on the guilt. How could he move forward when his late wife was in the ground?

"You should go," she said.

He hadn't meant to say the wrong thing. He was trying to spare her the embarrassment and the responsibility, but he had only made things worse.

"Will you be alright in the storm?" He didn't want to leave her here alone if she was still afraid. The rain still smacked against the house with force and the wind howled as if in pain.

"I'm fine. Thank you." She shuffled out of the room, probably toward the door.

He navigated through the dark as best he could, but still bumped into furniture. Something hard banged his shin. He bit back a curse. He deserved that and more.

She opened the door and the cool, wet air swooped in. The smell of rain filled the room. He could make her out in the flash of light from the sky. Her head was down. She stared at the ground.

"Will you be in class tomorrow?" He stood before her, not blaming her if she never wanted to see him again. He had made a fool of himself.

"Yes." She still didn't look at him, and it killed him.

"I truly am sorry, Petra. I'm not ready—"

"Just go, Mav. Please go."

His name on her lips excited him and made his heart ache. "Goodbye, then."

He stepped onto the porch and was hit with the rain. The door closed behind him with a soft click. He took his time getting into his car and was drenched through when he slid behind the wheel. But he couldn't feel the cold from the rain or even if his clothes were sticking to him. He was numb. And for the first time he wasn't sure if it was because of what he had done to Shelby or what he just did to Petra.

Petra sank against the door. The darkness pressed in on her. She wanted to run, run away from here, from the life she had built, from all her responsibilities. Instead, she slid to the floor and hugged her knees to her chest.

The power was out and could be that way for a while. Candlewood Falls wasn't exactly the first stop on the electric company's fix-it list. Maybe up on Main Street where all the shops were, but not out here. She would most likely sit right where she was until the power came back on or until morning. Whichever came first.

How could she have been so stupid to throw herself at Mav? Admittedly, she had been frightened when the lights went out and the thunder rattled her teeth. But when he pressed his lips against hers, it was as if everything had made sense for the first time in a long time.

She had almost thanked the stars above for the storm and bringing him to her. But then he got spooked or she was a bad kisser or whatever. She shook the thoughts from her head. She didn't want to know. Her cheeks burned hot with embarrassment.

"You need to pull yourself together and get up." Her voice echoed off the walls. She needed to hear something other than the rain. She pushed off the floor, annoyed with herself, and rummaged through the junk drawer in the kitchen.

She found matches to light the candle on the counter and a very large and heavy flashlight. Her father liked to have the right tools for everything.

At least with the flashlight on she could see where she was going. And she needed to get upstairs. She grabbed her mother's note and reread it. Her mom was right. She needed a life. A real life. With friends and people in it who wanted to be with her. She was tired of being the consolation prize. The second choice or the last resort choice like she felt around Paige.

Paige surely would have chosen to live with Frank so she could have stayed in her old town. Her friends were there. Even her job. But she had been forced to live with Petra, and Paige had made it clear she hadn't wanted that.

Petra marched into her parents' room, still untouched from the last time she was in here. Even though the drawers and closet were empty, the bathroom was still filled with oils and lotions. Soaps and sprays. She would start there.

Her movements were quick and hasty. She tossed things without regard into the box until it was too heavy to move. But all the drawers on her mother's side were empty. Most of the toiletries in the linen closet were gone too. She doubted her father would desire root touch-up or half-empty jars of makeup remover.

She dragged the box to the steps. How was she going to get it down the stairs? And to where? The garbage she supposed. Sweat trickled down her back and her breath came in short waves. All the adrenaline seeped from her body, and she sank onto the top step.

"Who am I kidding?" How was she going to show up at class tomorrow after what just happened? The packing had done nothing to calm the frustration and the humilia-tion. In fact, it had only made her realize how empty her life actually was.

She dug her phone out of her pocket and pulled up Ember's number. The call went to voicemail. She hung up without leaving a message.

The rain's beat slowed to a light drum. The thunder had made its way into the distance, torturing some other person or town. She should be glad she was safe, just like when her mom had found her under the boardwalk.

But like that time, all that swam inside her was regret. She had regretted not getting to Nyx in time without getting lost. And now she regretted not spending more time with her mom before it was too late.

She also regretted not leaving Frank sooner. And all the mistakes she had made with Paige.

She should regret kissing Mav.

But ironically, she did not.

In fact, if given the chance, she would do it again.

CHAPTER THIRTEEN

"Good morning, class," Mav said as he walked through the door. He had deliberately arrived ten minutes late. He had wanted all the students to already be there. He didn't want to risk bumping into Petra in the parking lot or along the corridor.

He hadn't been able to sleep at all last night. Thoughts of her had swarmed him and he couldn't swat a single one away. He had led her on, implying he wanted something with that kiss. Oh, he did all right. He wanted that kiss and for a brief second, he wanted all that could come after it.

But it couldn't happen. He was damaged goods and he would only end up hurting her in the end. He was doing her a favor. She just didn't know it yet.

"We're going to begin with making grilled eggplant sandwiches. It's an easy lunch option and a stepping stone to our competition meals. We only have a few weeks, so let's get cooking." He tried to put a lightness and enthusiasm in his voice that he didn't feel. He was afraid his students were onto him. His heart wasn't in this competition, and it wasn't in teaching. He could pretend all he wanted, but that was the honest truth.

Niko arched his brow as if he were trying to translate what Mav was saying. Titi's usual positive attitude hadn't arrived at class yet. She sulked in her seat. And Petra would not make eye contact. At least she had shown up. He had half expected her not to. And he wouldn't have blamed her.

They each took a spot at the counter of one of the kitchens and followed his directions. He would have each of them make today's menu to see who had what strengths. Then he would play to those strengths in the competition. They sliced eggplant and sprinkled garlic. They grilled the tomatoes and spread the bottom of the ciabatta bread with cheese.

Forty minutes later he did a taste test.

"Well?" Titi looked over his shoulder with anticipation. Her flowery-scented perfume clogged his nose and his taste buds. He might have to tell her not to wear that on the competition day.

He chewed and swallowed, but refrained from making any comments. He didn't have a whole lot to say, and he didn't have the energy to find the right words. He moved on to Niko's without feedback as well. Niko's sandwich had all the flavor, but the eggplant was soggy and the bread was blackened on the edges.

He stood before Petra's sandwich. She had cut the bread on a diagonal and decorated the plate with some kettle style chips. Nice touch. The bright red of the tomato complimented the earthy color of the eggplant.

The goat cheese peeked out of the back of the bread, just begging to be eaten.

He wanted to swipe the cheese with his finger and imagined what Petra would look like if she were to suck it off his finger. He dropped the fork he didn't know he was holding.

"It can't be that bad. You haven't even tried it yet," Petra said. Her eyes were the color of a stormy sky. And that thought drove him right back to last night. His head hurt.

"It looks great." He forced himself to take a bite. He wasn't hungry, and he was already tired of eating the sandwiches with no flavor. It was such a simple recipe and yet Niko and Titi seemed to have missed the mark.

With a deep breath, he took a bite. The burst of flavors from Petra's sandwich woke up his mouth. He could taste the fresh basil and the salt and pepper. The tomatoes added a lighter touch and a juiciness against the crusty warm bread. Now he had to force himself to put the sandwich down and not lick his damn fingers.

"Very good." Was all he could manage. He didn't want to rave about how fantastic it was because he didn't want her to think he was overcompensating for last night's debacle. But he could have raved about her presentation. He wasn't confusing his feelings for her with her ability to grill eggplant.

"Thank you." Her voice was soft and she toyed with the silver bracelet on her arm.

"You didn't say anything about mine," Titi said.

"It was a test run. We'll try it again. Don't worry. Everyone will improve. Let's clean up."

Niko shrugged. "Kind of hard to mess up a sandwich. What else could we have done differently?"

They had succeeded in following his directions, but something was missing. "How about if I make a quick sandwich too and you can taste the difference? Learn by example kind of thing."

He threw together the ingredients and grilled up the veggies in half the time his students had, but he wasn't judging them too harshly for that. They would need to get faster if they were going to have any chance of winning. He stopped. Did he actually care if they won or not? He almost laughed. Look at him, caring for a brief second.

He cut the sandwich into thirds and handed out the pieces. Titi groaned with pleasure. Niko gave him a thumbs-up. Tomato juice ran down Petra's chin. She wiped it away with her hand. She was beautiful with food on her face and a smile in her eyes. She had let her guard down for the briefest of seconds, and he could imagine her fully enjoying herself. He wished he could've seen her eyes last night. Were they full of lust before he had doused them with his abrupt change of direction?

He handed Petra a napkin, but she waved him off.

"You're a mess, sweetie." Titi also handed her one. This time Petra took it. He hoped his face didn't give away the disappointment he felt.

"That tomato. How did you get it to taste like that?" she said, licking the side of her hand. Petra finally looked at him. Her eyes were bright with delight.

"I know," Titi said. "I cut my slice from the same one, and it didn't taste that way."

"It's in the seasonings. You'll get the hang of it." That wasn't the whole truth. He had watched each of them as they seasoned and assembled the food. But only Petra's was full of flavor. Some people were born to be chefs, and others had to work hard at it. Passion trumped talent, but the gifted ones had to have an ounce of passion for their gifts to come through in the flavors. Petra had passion. He knew that much now.

"Looks like time is up for today." Petra pointed at the clock over the door.

"See you all tomorrow." Niko swaggered out of the class.

"I've got to run. Busy day." Titi ran after Niko.

Petra gathered the cutting boards and knives, placing them in one of the sinks. She kept her back to him as she wiped down a counter.

"You don't have to do that," he said.

"It's not a big deal. The other two left in a hurry." She shrugged and went back to the task.

"Can I talk to you for a second?" He needed to apologize if she would allow him.

"There's nothing to talk about, really. I'll just clean up and be on my way. You don't even have to stay if you're uncomfortable."

"Me?" He couldn't stand that she wouldn't look at him. He put his hand over hers with the sponge. Her gaze snapped up. "Please let me at least explain."

She eased away from him. "We got caught up in the moment. The storm... and it was dark... and I threw myself in your arms." She turned her back to him. "I can understand that you thought I wanted to kiss you. You were just being nice."

"Is that what you think?" Embarrassed laughter

bubbled right at the top of his throat. She was so far off the mark he couldn't help but want to laugh. He was the pathetic one, running from his feelings for her.

She spun around. Fire burned in her blue eyes. "Why else would you have kissed me?" She kept her voice at a low-level hiss. "Clearly, you hadn't wanted to. You couldn't get out of my house fast enough."

That part was true. He had wanted to run as far and as fast as he could because he couldn't handle his reaction to her. He had wanted to carry her upstairs and make love to her all night long. He sure as hell wanted that kiss.

"I didn't kiss you because I felt sorry for you," he said, trying to make her understand.

"Oh, please, Mav. I may be out of practice, but I'm not a fool. There is a difference between a man who wants a woman and one who doesn't. Unless you don't like women in a sexual way. All you had to do was say you were gay."

He tried not to laugh again. "I'm not gay, Petra."

"Involved with someone else, then?"

"Not exactly." He shoved his hands in his pockets because he didn't know what to do with them.

"I knew it." She grabbed her very large purse and slung it over her shoulder. "We have another few weeks together. Let's just keep to the cooking, and we'll get through this. Okay?"

"Not okay." He was about to agree with her, but different words came bursting out of his mouth. She was right. If they remained professional, the next weeks would go by without too much trouble, and then he would probably never see her again.

"What do you mean, *not okay*?"

"I mean... I want to kiss you again." He hadn't meant to say that either. Oh, yes, he did. He meant it in every part of his body. And that scared the hell out of him.

"Forget it, Maverick. You can't kiss me. Now or ever." She marched for the door.

But before she could cross the doorway, he said, "Are you sure?"

She spun around, the anger gone from her eyes. "No, I'm not sure. But I'm leaving anyway."

"Before you go, just tell me you know that I didn't kiss you because I felt sorry for you last night." He could live with that much. He had no right to ask for more.

"I don't know that. I don't know why you kissed me." She crossed her arms over her chest. He should just let her go. Her body language said she wanted out, but her eyes... said something else. Her eyes always gave her away.

"I kissed you because I couldn't stop myself. Because I like you. Because of a whole host of reasons I haven't worked through yet," he said.

"How are you going to work through these reasons of yours?" She tightened her arms around her chest and clenched her jaw. Looked like she wasn't going to give him an inch.

"By kissing you again. If you'll allow me to."

"And what about this class and my grade?" She took a step into the classroom.

"Your grade has nothing to do with whether or not you kiss me. You'll probably get an A because so far you seem to be the only one who can cook anything." She had a magic most people didn't have. A gift. She just didn't know it yet. He wanted to show it to her, though.

"We've only made a sandwich." She narrowed her eyes.

"Trust me. I can usually tell right away who's got the chops or not." Not everyone who wanted to be a professional cook should be. He'd watched many people leave the kitchen with their tails between their legs.

"So if I say no to us kissing again, I will get the grade I deserve?" She continued to come closer. Maybe she wasn't as mad as she had been.

"Absolutely. I've got no reason to lie. If you never speak to me again outside of this room, I swear you will get the grade you earned. My pride might be bruised, but my scruples are firmly in place." He would never take advantage of her or any woman. He was a lot of things, but he wasn't a perv or a man who abused his power. He had made it his mission to treat all his employees with the respect they deserved.

"Taking this class is more than I bargained for." She dropped her hands to her sides.

"I hope that's a good thing." He took a step toward her. She didn't run away.

"I haven't decided yet," she said with her lips pressed into a thin line.

"When you do, will you let me know?" The space between them frizzled with heat. She was going to be the end of him. He couldn't fight this feeling for her. And he didn't want to.

"I will," she said with a breathlessness.

"So, can I kiss you again?" He inched closer, taking his

time, enjoying the chemistry between them. He wanted to drag out this new sensation that was making his shorts snug.

"We'll see." She spun on her heel and darted out the door without a look back.

CHAPTER FOURTEEN

"Liar, liar, pants on fire." Ember slapped her arm.

"Hey." She rubbed the spot on her skin that smarted. They walked down Main Street. She gripped an iced coffee in her hand from the Green Bean. The sun sat plump and full in the sky. The day was already heating up as if the storm two days ago had never been a thing. That was summer in New Jersey. Sticky with humidity like honey on a bun.

The sidewalk was filled with summer visitors who came to see the red mill and the shops along Main Street. Families sat on benches having a light breakfast, even ice cream already. She had asked Ember to meet with her before her class began.

"I'm not lying." Okay, she was a little.

"Petra, you might be able to fool your teacher, but you can't fool me. I know that goofy smirk on your face. It's the same look you got when you were fifteen and Mark Sampson kissed you for the first time down the street from our house so Dad wouldn't find out."

She remembered that night. Mark had been in her study hall, but she hadn't noticed him until he had come to the orchard one night in late November. The orchard had been holding an evening event, and he was with his friends. The group of boys had been laughing and tumbling over each other as if they were puppies. She had made a snarky comment and adorable Mark Sampson had swaggered right up to her. He hadn't kissed her that night. It wasn't for a few weeks later. She smiled in spite of herself. She had had a mad crush on that boy. Her feelings for Mav were very different. They were adult mad crush feelings.

"Fine. I do want to kiss him again. There. I said it. Now what? How do I go back to class, knowing the only thing I'll be thinking about is kissing him? I didn't sign up for that class to find a boyfriend. I wanted to find myself."

They paused outside the Witchy Woman store and gazed at the window. This shop was newer and she wasn't as familiar with it as some of the others. The owner did readings and sold crystals and stuff. And was dating her cousin Sam.

"We should get our fortunes told." Ember jumped on her toes.

"No, thanks. I don't want to know what the future holds." Unless it included a new career for her. And maybe an answer about Mav.

"Fine. Another time." Ember linked their arms, and they continued their jaunt. "How is the packing coming?"

"Slow." Probably too slow.

"Did Dad say when he would be back?"

"By Labor Day. He said Paige and I could stay at the house after he returned if we wanted, but I don't think so." Living with her father was the last thing she had in mind when she thought about reinventing herself. But the rent was good for now. He had no plans of charging her. He had said as much. She had been surprised by his admission, but her father was a man of his word. She doubted he would change his mind on that. Still, she didn't want to live with him.

"Will you live there?" Ember asked as if reading her mind.

"I need a job before I can rent a place. I was hoping this cooking class would give me enough skills to get employment in a restaurant."

"Why won't you consider opening a little café on the orchard?" When Ember got an idea in her head, she would not let it go.

"Not this again. Dad will never allow it." But the kernel stuck in her mind. The café could be something of her own. The first thing that was completely hers. Well, not completely. It would be on the family orchard. But wasn't that orchard partly hers? No one had kept her from working there, only owning it. She had been the one who had wanted a life outside of Candlewood Falls. Foolishly believing something better waited for her over the county line. She may have been wrong about that. This town was in her blood. It called to her.

"But Brad was interested. Have you spoken to him about it any more?"

"He wasn't serious." But that day in the coffee shop, he had appeared to be considering it.

"Brad is earnest about business. Don't let the pink nail polish fool you," Ember hollered with laughter.

"Pink nail polish? Brad doesn't exactly look the type."

Not with all those muscles and the glare in his eye she had witnessed over the years. He was intense. Maybe because he had to be with all those people working for him. The orchard was hard work. Brad and his sister had grown up tough too. Uncle Silas raised them in a two-room cabin with no running water. She didn't know how they had managed. She would've hated every second of that.

"You haven't noticed? His daughter is ten. She loves pink. He lets her paint his nails when she wants to. It's hysterical. Raf teases him all the time, but Raf loves it too. He wants a child of his own. Don't say anything to anyone, but we're talking about it."

"What?" She stopped in her tracks. She hadn't meant to yell. The surprise announcement took her off-balance. Ember had never mentioned wanting kids before.

"Shh. The town doesn't need to know. He has always wanted a family of his own. He has his brothers, and he practically raised them, but he's been talking about him and me having a child. I don't know, what do you think about me being a mom?"

"You're in your forties."

"Does that mean I'd make a bad mom?" Hurt passed over Ember's blue eyes. She wanted to kick herself.

"You'd be a great mom. But don't you think having a baby in your forties is kind of old to get started?" She couldn't imagine having a baby now at forty-three. Children sucked energy like an inefficient air conditioner. Starting late wouldn't give Ember the advantage of bouncing back easily like being younger would.

"I never wanted children the way you did. You knew you wanted to be a mom when we were in high school.

Don't you remember what you told your guidance counselor?"

Mr. Valen had asked her what she wanted to be at the beginning of her senior year. She had clamped her mouth closed around the word chef because her father had already shot that idea down. She had no other thoughts about her future that day other than to have a family where she would have people who loved her for her.

"I was a kid. I had no idea how hard it would be to raise a child."

"I can only imagine, but with Raf, I can do anything. He and I make a good team, and with what just happened to Mom, I don't want to waste any more time. We don't know how long we have. I've taken life for granted too long. I need to take more action."

"Action? All you do is take action. You never think things all the way through. You've only been with Raf a few months. Don't you think you should get to know him better before you have a child? You can't get rid of him once a baby is in the picture."

Ember glared at her. "Why would I want to get rid of him? I love him. He's the best thing that has ever happened to me. He's my rock. He's strong and responsible. He loves my impulsiveness."

"You don't know what it's like to be a parent. You can't undo it once it's done." She didn't regret being a mother, but there had been times when the reward didn't outweigh the effort. When her teenager looked at her as if she were a stranger, or worse a monster, a piece of her died inside. She didn't expect to be repaid—motherhood wasn't that kind of job—but she did want a little appreciation. That seemed impossible to achieve. The lack of it hurt worse than a knife through her chest. And Ember was ready to jump in with both feet, not caring about the long-term results or how hard it would be to raise a child alone if things didn't work out for her and her man.

Ember placed her hands on her Petra's shoulders. "I'm ready to take the chance. I'm ready to build a family with the man I love and who loves me more than I can imagine. Yes, things between him and me happened quickly, but it's as real as I am standing here with you. Petra, I love you, but it's time you started taking a few chances of your own. Kiss your teacher. Please for me, do more than kiss him."

She eased away from Ember's grip. The heat and the thick air turned her stomach. She tossed her iced coffee in the nearby garbage can. She wasn't Ember. She couldn't live her life on a whim. And Ember shouldn't bring a child into the world on a whim either.

Instead of saying that, she said, "I have to get to class. Thanks for the walk."

"Petra, wait," Ember called after her.

She kept walking as the only way to keep the prickly monster in her throat at bay. It seemed Ember was always on to the next stage of her life, and she was stuck behind. It didn't seem fair.

She drove to the college and parked in the student lot. The tan brick building where they had class squatted at the other end of the cracked and faded asphalt. The campus was plain except for the building with the administrative offices. The school didn't have that historical quality made complete by tall red brick buildings with columns. That look was saved for four-year schools with histories dating back to the revolution. The community college had been built in the nineteen-seventies when the county had expanded and more people had moved out west from the city.

Some trees lined the perimeter of the parking lot and swayed in the light breeze that did nothing to cool the morning down. A small grassy area with some picnic benches was in the near distance. A few students sat there talking and laughing as if they didn't have a care in the world.

She sat in her car, unsure of what to do next. She wanted to go in and learn today's recipe. Mav had paid her a lovely compliment by saying her sandwich was the only one with flavor. She had done exactly what he had said, so she didn't completely understand why her food tasted better. But when her hands cut and chopped and sprinkled seasoning, her chest had felt as if it had opened up and she had sprouted wings and could fly. She was free when her hands were creating with food.

But she also didn't want to go inside and see him. Her feelings had confused her. Her job here in Candlewood Falls was to pack up her mom's things and she hadn't done enough of it. Instead, she had selfishly signed up for a class. Her father would be home in no time at all, and she would have to find a place to stay. Did that mean in Candlewood Falls? But she couldn't move Paige again. That wasn't fair.

Paige was still fighting her on taking classes this fall. She held out hope Paige would change her mind. But what would that solve for her?

Titi ran by her car and waved. She pointed to the building. Petra gave the one minute sign and Titi ran ahead, nodding. Someone knocked on the window and she jumped.

Mav leaned down and smiled at her. "I can't teach the class out here," he said through the closed window.

"I'll be right in." She turned off the car.

"I'll wait." He leaned his back against the car door, giving her full view of his broad shoulders and tapered waist. What if she channeled Ember and leaped without looking? She could kiss Mav again and maybe allow herself to taste him in other places. If he was still interested.

She shook her head and pushed out of the car, making him buck forward. "You're very bossy." But she liked that he had wanted to wait for her. And she liked his teasing.

"That's what I've been told."

"What do you want, Mav?" She would still need to have some boundaries, or at least a few rules to this game between them. She couldn't change completely in one afternoon.

"I want to walk you to class." He shrugged one shoulder.

"That's it?" She wasn't expecting such a simple answer.

"That's it."

She pushed her disappointment down. She wanted him to say he had thought of nothing but kissing her again. If he had said that, she would have given her permission this time.

He didn't say anything else so she headed for the building. He fell into step beside her, keeping pace. She wondered if he had to slow down because of those long legs. He had her paying attention in a way she hadn't ever.

Her gaze would search him out in the classroom or when he was nearby until she sensed that current under her skin.

"Can I ask you something?" She valued his opinion. He had admirable success once even if he had lost it. He would still be the right person to ask advice about her café idea.

"Sure." He smiled down at her, blocking some of the sun with his height. His physical presence was as much of a comfort as talking with him was. Oh, she was falling for him. How did she let this happen?

"Petra, where did you go?" Mav waved a hand in front of her face.

"I'm sorry. Runaway thoughts. That seems to happen more and more. Okay, here goes. How did you know you wanted your own restaurant?"

He shoved his hands in his pockets and kept walking. They took a turn on the footpath heading away from the building. "We have a few minutes. Do you mind if we keep going?" he said.

"I'd like that." Spending time alone with him was nice. She didn't need to be inside with the others where she would have to share him.

"Well, when I worked for other people, I always wanted to do things my way. I had so many ideas and most chefs didn't want to hear them. They had ideas of their own, and the customers were coming for the head chef. I can't say I blame them, but I realized I didn't need them."

If she had her own place—dare she say it, like the café —she could make her own decisions too. She would prob- ably have to run some things by Brad and her father and her uncle and her cousins... Too many people to have to report to. She would never be allowed to have complete control of a café on the orchard—and that was what she needed. Control.

"What cooking school did you go to?" She would gather more information before she went shooting her mouth off about crazy ideas like owning cafes.

He barked out a laugh. "Cooking school? No, ma'am. I am a hands-on kind of guy. I learned on my own, by watching others, and by making a ton of mistakes."

So, maybe she didn't need to have a certificate or a degree to cook professionally. If he could do it, why not her too? "How did you get people to hire you?"

"I can be very persuasive when I want to be." He smirked.

The heat climbed into her face. She didn't doubt that one bit. Not with that devilish smile and the twinkle in his dark eyes. The path looped around and brought them back to the front of the building with its short staircase and glass doors.

"What's with the questions?" He stopped by the steps, not going inside.

She took his cue and stayed put too. "Just curious. I guess."

"Are you thinking of working in a restaurant?"

"Maybe." She hadn't voiced that to anyone yet. She had been protecting that idea because it was so vulnerable, like a new plant needing love and attention.

"Don't do it, Petra. It's nothing but heartache. Take what you learn here and cook for yourself. You'll never be happy cooking for anyone else. Trust me. I know." He checked his phone. "We should get inside." He jogged up the steps and held the door for her.

"I need a minute. I'll be in soon." She fought to keep the wobble out of her voice.

"Don't be late." He laughed as if he didn't have a care in the world or as if he hadn't stomped on her tender idea.

She held completely still.

Except for the one tear that slipped down her cheek and off her chin.

CHAPTER FIFTEEN

"No. No. No. You're murdering the chicken." Mav slapped his hand against his head. It was chicken for crying out loud. It wasn't that hard to make chicken And still each one of them couldn't do it. Even Petra was off her game. Maybe the sandwich was just beginner's luck. Of course, it was. What the hell had he been thinking?

Titi held the meat mallet in the air, poised and ready to slam it down on the defenseless thigh like the killer in a slasher movie. Her eyes were as wide as a two-pound can of beans.

"Don't look so surprised," Niko said to Titi. "You've been beating the crap out of that thing for five minutes."

"It won't flatten," she said.

"Titi, sauté the spinach—but only until it's soft." She could do less damage with that. He needed a break. "I'll be right back." He stole a glance at Petra who had pulled her hair back. Small wisps fell around her face. She pushed her bottom lip out and blew away the strands that wouldn't stay put.

She had been quiet since she had come in. He shouldn't have told her not to work in a restaurant. He was just trying to spare her some of the heartache he had been through, without telling his story. She reminded him now of a tall reed in the grass. One hard wind would come along and flatten her. The restaurant business was not for the light at heart. It was competitive and sometimes vindictive once the stakes were high enough.

He pushed out into the summer heat and wiped a hand over his face. His three students weren't equipped to compete. He had made a mistake entering them in the contest. Would he do more damage by pulling the plug on them, telling them he thought they were terrible cooks, or would he be doing them a favor?

"Mav?" Petra stood behind him. Her hands were on her hips and her brows were knitted. He bit back the joke about the crease between her eyes. She didn't look as if she were in the mood for his humor.

"I'll be right in. Can you tell the others to start cleaning up?" Class was almost over and he was ready to call it quits for the day. He had a lot to figure out.

"You have to be more supportive of what we're doing. We don't know how to cook and you've given us a recipe that was above our capabilities. You're setting us up to fail."

"Is that what you think?"

"I think that you have unrealistic expectations. And after your comment to me earlier, I also think you don't like cooking anymore. Which is fine, but why take this job? Why take away our chance to learn something about ourselves if you were so against it in the first place?"

"I don't know."

"Somehow I doubt that. There's something deep about you. I can feel it when you aren't in the classroom. It's like you're a different person. When you're here, you are not here." She tapped her head.

"Petra, you don't know what you're talking about." She had hit so close to home it sent a shudder over his skin.

"When you decide you want to actually be the teacher and help us, then let us know. In the meantime, I'll be bringing in tomorrow's recipe for us to practice. If we're going to be forced to compete, at the very least we need a chance." She headed back inside without waiting for him to respond.

He wanted to kick something, but there wasn't even a pebble in sight. He would get in his car and get as far away from this place as possible. If Petra wanted to bring in the recipe, then she could have at it. He sure as hell didn't need to. She could teach the damn class. He suspected that without much effort, she would be better than him in no time anyway.

His phone buzzed in his pocket. He was tempted to ignore it, but it could be Bash so he dug it out of his pocket. Not Bash. Avery. "Hey, Avery. What's up?"

"I have amazing news."

"Yeah, what's that?" He hit the key fob to unlock his car door.

"The school is on board with a culinary arts program. We have some alumni who are in the field and love the idea. They want to donate a boatload of money to make it happen. I told them you were teaching the summer trial class. They were so excited. They want you to teach three sections this fall and possibly next spring. Isn't that great?"

"That's terrible. I'm not coming out of retirement to teach." He slid into the car and kicked it over, opening the windows and letting the oppressive heat out. He wished someone could let the oppressiveness out of him too.

"Oh, come on, Mav. This is the best news ever. You could make a comeback with this."

"I don't want to cook anymore." When were the people in his life going to understand that?

"You're so full of it."

"Avery, I have to go." He ended the call without warning. He acted like a jerk, but he couldn't have that conversation on top of the one he just had with Petra. When he had seen Petra in her car earlier, he had actually believed he would have a good day. She had agreed to walk with him, had asked him advice even. Then he had gone and stuck his foot in his mouth; his students are the worst apprentices he'd ever had, and now Avery wanted him to be a regular teacher.

He shot a text to Bash.

Can you meet for lunch?

I'm at your little apartment. Good enough?

Fine. Be there in a few. See if Clark wants to join.

Will do.

At least Bash would be on his side. He could always count on Bash to have his back.

∾

Mav inhaled the salty smell of the grilled salmon. He sliced it and put it on hard rolls with butter lettuce, tomato, red onion, and a chipotle mayo. His mouth watered.

The grill's fire made sweat run down his face, but an unexpected breeze had picked up. Another storm was probably on the way. He would check the weather app after lunch. And he would not check on Petra. She was so damn independent. She sure as hell didn't need him.

He and Bash sat outside at the wood picnic table Clark had near the garage. The table was old and faded with splintered wood, but he needed to be outdoors.

The apartment had felt too small the second he had returned from school. He couldn't breathe in such close quarters. That had always been his problem. He needed space and air. Staying in Candlewood Falls for too long seemed like a life sentence at the moment even with its expanse and rolling hills. Only when he was with Petra did the frenetic energy in his veins calm. He squeezed his eyes shut. No more thoughts about Petra and how she made him feel.

Clark opened the back door of his house and stuck out his head. "Boys, I'm passing on lunch. My granddaughter just called me on one of those video things."

"Aren't you going to eat?" Mav held a plate up.

"I didn't say I wasn't going to eat. Bring that here, foolish young man." Clark waved him over.

Bash laughed. He shot Bash a glare, who quickly shut up, and gave the food to Clark.

"Do you want me to come over later and help with the kitchen?"

"Mav, I appreciate the help. I do. But I've decided to

hire a contractor. New guy in town. Name's Tony. Needs the work."

"Grandpa, are you there?" a young female voice squealed from inside the house.

"Gotta run. Thanks for the food." Clark held up the plate and closed the door. Mav returned to his brother.

"I like him," Bash said.

"Yeah, me too."

"Avery's right, you know." Bash tucked a napkin into the collar of his shirt.

"Avery is one hundred percent wrong." He put the plate in front of his brother.

Bash clamped his mouth around the sandwich and dug in. "Look, you're the only one who believes your cooking days are over," Bash said in between chews.

He wasn't hungry any longer, if he ever was. He had just wanted to get off the campus and do something that made the tightness in his chest disappear. "I'm keeping it simple these days."

"You're playing it safe."

"Every time I consider going back into the business, I think of the last time I spoke to Shelby. I lost everything to cook food for other people. How could I have been so stupid?"

Bash placed the sandwich on the table with deliberation and wiped his hands. "Wanting to make something of yourself isn't a crime. You were driven. Hell, I'm driven. Sacrifices get made sometimes."

"Are you saying losing Shelby was a necessary sacrifice?"

"Fuck no." Bash shook his head. "What I'm trying to say is sometimes relationships suffer for the price of success. You weren't just cooking food. You were running a very successful business. You employed many people. You brought enjoyment to other people when they needed it. And you were the best at it. No matter what I say, no one can be good at everything. Not even me. I think I'm learning that."

"It seems wrong to be a success when Shelby isn't even here. It isn't fair."

"Giving up your life isn't the answer. It won't bring Shelby back." Bash took another messy bite of his food.

"But teaching..." Teaching in a classroom had never been the plan. But plans change. Teaching would be a way to start slow, work his way back to the restaurant business. Or teaching could suck the joy of cooking out of him once and for all.

"I wasn't sure if I should bring this up," Bash said. "But if you want to say screw it to the teaching gig, I have an opportunity for you."

"What are you talking about?" He couldn't completely walk away from teaching. He had promised Avery to finish the summer class. He had to at least get them to the end of that.

"I've been approached to invest in a restaurant. A buddy of mine wants to open a farm-to-table concept." Bash continued to massacre his food.

"So?"

"So... I said I would invest if you could be the chef." Bash cracked open his beer. The plume of steam from the cold beer hitting the warm air floated from the bottle's neck. Bash took a big swig as if he hadn't just said the most insane thing in ages.

"Why would you do that? How could you use me as a

pawn in your negotiations? I should beat the crap out of you for that."

"Listen, drama queen, no one was using you. Not really anyway. You need to get off your ass and do something that brings you some enjoyment. And I don't like investing in anything unless I can minimize the risks. You are the best chef on the East Coast."

"Cooking doesn't fulfill me anymore."

"Neither does that warehouse job you've been doing either. Look, this is an upstart opportunity. You could be involved in picking the location. This Candlewood Falls place is pretty nice. Farms are around every corner here. You could offer real farm-to-fork menus. You could change them every season. And doesn't your Petra's family own an orchard?"

"How do you know that?"

Bash smirked. "Man, I do my research. It wasn't that hard to figure out. You could use the orchard for your fruit needs. They have apples and pumpkins. I bet you could get them to plant some berries. Who knows what else? That's your area."

"I don't want to be used, Bash." And Petra wasn't his. She would never want him.

"This is a real business opportunity for both of us. And none of the risk is on you this time. You'd be involved in every stage of development including hiring the staff. Not one penny of yours would be on the line."

"You arranged all of this already?" Bash never waited for permission. He always went ahead and did whatever he wanted and let the consequences fall where they may. More often than not, Bash got what he wanted.

"I have the contract," Bash took another swig of beer.

"That's why you came out here. It had nothing to do with Jess."

"Oh, no. Jess has a lot to do with this. She and I are through, and I did want to see you. You're still the person I need when my life blows up."

And Bash had been there for him when his life had exploded. "Thanks, but I think you would have bounced back. Did you even really love Jess?"

"Who knows? She says I only love money. I don't think that's a total truth."

"Only half-true," he said.

"Listen, I could've told you about this restaurant thing on the phone. I didn't because I wanted to spend more time with you. And I wanted to see Candlewood Falls. I like this town. It's got something. Homey, I think. I could stay here."

"It's alright." The hometown feel had appealed to him too, but he didn't want to say that just yet. Bash would think he'd won the argument. And he hadn't. Mav wasn't ready to agree to anything. Not even something that had an ounce of appeal.

Bash arched a brow. "What do you say, Mav? Will you take the offer?"

"I don't know. I have Avery to consider. I don't want to be the reason she loses her job. And this competition. I can't pull the class from it. When does he, this friend of yours, want to open his place?"

"By late spring. He wants to be ready when all the good veggies start to become available. I can set up a meeting with him."

"I don't want to be rushed into anything."

"Ask Petra what she thinks." Bash returned to his sandwich, tearing at it with his teeth and lips.

Petra was mad at him. The only thing she would think about him was how fast she could get away from him. But he would like to know what she thought about this idea. Bash was crazy for setting it up, for even thinking it, but something fluttered in his belly. Something familiar and foreign. Was he out of his mind for even entertaining the idea of having complete control of a restaurant again? A farm-to-table establishment could be kept small to keep costs down, but it would create excitement for locals. And Candlewood Falls didn't have a restaurant like that. He had checked because he couldn't help himself. He had kept himself informed about the industry. Just because.

"I need to go. I'll be back later." He wrapped up his portion in tinfoil. Maybe he'd be hungry later.

"You're making dinner, right?" Bash wiped his face with the napkin still tucked in his shirt.

"You're eating lunch. Why are you worried about dinner already?"

"Because only my big brother makes anything worth eating. I don't want to miss it." Bash smiled with the mayo on his lip the napkin missed. "You're going to Petra's, right?"

"Stop asking about her." If she would see him. Maybe he should bring a bottle of wine and a fruit tart. He'd seen one in the grocery store that looked pretty good.

"You have that determined look in your eye. It's good to see it's back." Bash pulled the napkin from his collar and crumpled it.

"Don't get ahead of yourself. I haven't agreed to anything. And I doubt I will. You just hit on something I had been considering before everything happened with Shelby." And Bash knew that. Bash wasn't stupid.

"Take your time and think about it," Bash said.

He paused near his car. "What if I fuck it all up again?"

Bash walked over and patted him on the shoulder. "And what if you don't?"

CHAPTER SIXTEEN

P etra had come home early from class today. She had left the cleanup to Titi and Niko. The anger had distracted her too much. Mav had treated them as if they were an inconvenience and not his students. Granted, Titi would test the patience of the best saint with her inability to follow directions, but he had no right to speak to her as if she were anything more than a gnat to be swatted at.

She studied a recipe of her mother's. The index card was yellowed and the corner turned. But her mom's handwriting was still clear. She had wanted to try it out and then teach it to Titi and Niko like she had threatened to do. But even this recipe would be too much for them. She couldn't coach any better than he could. She would drop the class tomorrow. The whole thing wasn't what she had signed up for. Especially not all the conflicting emotions for Mav.

Petra had gone to him asking for advice and guidance, maybe a little reassurance, this morning, thinking he would have the sage counsel she needed, and he had smashed her hopes in one fell swoop. Even now the anger twisted inside her like a congealed spaghetti.

"Mom, have you seen this?" Paige pounded up the basement steps and into the kitchen holding a fat photo album. Dirt streaked her cheek and dust covered her t-shirt and shorts.

"I don't think so." She hadn't even attempted to pack up the basement yet. She had taken one look at all the boxes and bags piled against the walls and turned around, running back upstairs. She hadn't returned.

"There must be a hundred or more photos in here." Paige flipped through the pages, sending tiny particles of dust spinning into the air.

"I'll take a look at that later. Since you're here, there's something I want to talk to you about." She had been trying to find the right time to discuss the fall semester, but Paige was always rushing out the door. Now seemed like as good a time as any.

"What is it?" Paige dropped the book on the counter with a thud.

"Have you given any more thought to the fall semester?"

"There isn't anything to think about. I'm not going. I don't need college." Paige set her jaw.

"What kind of a career do you think you'll have without an education?"

"Plenty of people have fulfilling careers without college. That will be me."

"You're making a mistake. You're hindering your earning potential. You'll have to work twice as hard to make the same." A tightness filled the bottom of her throat. She had to make Paige understand.

"It's my life. If I decide to go to college when I'm thirty, then I'll go." Paige threw her hands in the air.

"Paige—"

"Mom, stop. Grandpa didn't go to college. He did just fine. Better than fine."

"The family business was already in place. He worked there as a kid. It's not the same thing." The tightness in her throat choked her words. She dropped onto the chair. How did she make Paige see reason?

"Then I'll work at the orchard until I decide what to do next. There's plenty for me to do."

"Like what? Pick apples with Junior?" The words were out in a flash and no matter how hard she reached, they were out of her grasp, a poison stinking up the air.

"You never ask me how I feel about things. You always assume you know, but you don't. All you have to do is ask me how I feel about college."

She didn't have the energy for this conversation. Not again. All she had ever tried to do was cater to Paige's feelings, telling her she was entitled to every one she had. She had stroked and coddled all of Paige's emotions every time she had one. And if she had missed a few times in the past nineteen years, so be it. She wasn't a perfect mother. But she tried. God help her, she tried.

She couldn't take another second of what someone else needed today. First Mav this morning with his outburst and now Paige. Petra had her own needs. When would someone meet them for her?

Her insides burned. "Just do as you're told for once. Just one single time stop arguing with me and trust that I know what I'm talking about."

Paige turned on her heel and headed out of the kitchen.

"You're not leaving until you see that you have to go to college." She jumped out of the chair, almost knocking it over.

"Watch me." Paige grabbed her phone and wallet. The front door slammed shut.

"Nice. Real nice," she said under her breath. She had handled that terribly and would have a lot to apologize for. She was screwing everything up.

She grabbed the photo album and sat back down. The wind had picked up and the sun had hidden behind some thick clouds. No storms were predicted for the rest of the day. She was grateful for the reprieve.

She flipped open the book. It was an old-style album with the plastic that went over the photos, permanently sticking them to the cardboard. The pages smelled damp and old. Most of them had browned around the edges.

But the photos were still rich. She flipped the pages quickly, then went back to the beginning. Every page had been signed at the bottom by her mother.

The photos were from a different time. Forty years earlier. Pictures of flowers seen through an artistic eye with blurred leaves and attention to the water droplets on the vibrant petals. Photos of the rolling hills she had seen out her windows growing up, and yet their majesty was like nothing she'd seen before. Her mother had taken shots of clouds rolling out to the ocean in an orange sky.

As Petra turned the pages, there were other photos, some not as well done. Photos of cars when they were oversized and made of metal. Almost none with people in it. Her mother had an incredible eye. She had no idea that her mother had ever had such talent or such a love for photography. Why had her mother kept this a secret?

The last couple of pages were photos of her father. In most of them, he looked away from the camera. He might not have known the camera was on him. But her mother had caught him, young, handsome, pensive. The photos stopped like a story without a proper ending.

She ran into the basement and scoured the piles for more albums. She tossed black garbage bags to the side without care. She searched the metal shelves that held everything from childhood toys to broken fans. She climbed around folding tables and cardboard boxes of who knew what. No other photo albums were anywhere.

Sweat ran down her back. She took a deep breath. "Why did you stop, Mom?"

She dragged herself back up the steps and into the kitchen. She needed some air and some space to process what she just found out.

She grabbed the album and her purse. The only place she could think to go was Ember's.

She hoped she wasn't busting in on any evening love-making, but she needed someone to talk to. Someone who might understand. She wanted to call Mav, but didn't.

The ride to Ember's went faster than she had antici-pated, but just long enough to discourage her from pulling into the driveway. She didn't have to tell her sisters what she had found. Her mother had never felt it necessary to share her past. But there was so much more going on for her. Her problem wasn't just the pictures. She drove around the block to get up the courage to face her fears.

"Stop being ridiculous," she said to the empty vehicle. And finally pulled in.

A pickup backed out of the drive toward her. The driver, noticing she blocked the way, slammed on the brakes. She hesitated. She could pull out again, but she would probably keep going and she needed to vent the thoughts making a tangled web of her mind.

Before she could decide to flee or stay, a tall man with a striking resemblance to the very handsome Andy Garcia hopped out.

"Can I help you?" he said, coming closer to her car. He wore a simple starched white button-down shirt with the sleeves rolled to his elbows and a pair of dark jeans.

She stuck her head out the window. "Hi. Sorry to block your way out. I'm here to visit my sister."

Ember and Raf lived on one side of a two-family house that Raf owned. Petra didn't know who Raf rented the other side out to, but most likely the handsome man with a dazzling smile.

"Ah, Ember's sister. Which one? The mother or the singer?" He had a small hint of a Spanish accent.

"I guess my sister speaks about us quite a bit. I'm the oldest one. Petra. And I have a daughter." She wanted to be more than the sister who was the mother.

"Nice to meet you, Petra. I am Johnny Alvarez, Rafael's father." Johnny held out his hand.

She slipped her hand into his strong, rough grip. "Nice to meet you too."

"I'll pull my truck back up and you can park to the right. Ember and Rafael are home. He must've had an early night at the orchard for a change. He usually isn't home before ten most nights."

"Do you think I'll be bothering them?" She was going

to interrupt some romantic dinner. She could feel it in her bones. She should just leave before Ember noticed her car.

"Family is never a bother. They will be happy to know you're here. I hope to see you again soon." He offered a small wave and pulled his truck up far enough for her to park behind Ember's little vehicle with her bakery decal on the side.

She waved again to Johnny as he pulled away, but she was stalling. Telling Ember was going to make her mother's past more real. And hers more uncertain.

"Petra, what are you doing out here?" Ember bounded out the front door in a pair of jogging shorts and a cropped tee. Her hair was piled up on her head and her face was void of makeup.

"I came to say hi." She slid out of the car before Ember could look in the window and see the photo album. "I hope it's okay."

"I was about to go for a run. Do you want to come?"

"Are you serious right now?" She didn't like to run and the humidity would kill her on the spot.

"Totally serious. I can't sit still anymore. Raf is in his shed carving wood. He says he needs to unwind after all the stress at work. I had other ideas, but apparently men need to be in the mood too." She pressed her lips into a thin line and shook her head.

"Jeez, Ember, spare me the possible visuals."

"Get over it, Petra. Raf and I have sex. Great sex. You should try it some time. Just not with Raf." Ember winked, knowing not one of them would ever dream of stealing the other's man. "I'm going to take a wild guess and say you never kissed your hot teacher again."

"I didn't come here to talk about Mav." Though she definitely had opinions about him at the moment.

"Is this serious?"

"I don't know. Probably not."

"You're kind of scaring me."

"I'll show you." She went back to the car and retrieved the album. "Take a look at this." She sat on the step. Her legs were too tired to hold her up.

Ember sat beside her and opened the book. "These are pretty. Who took—Mom?" Ember stared at her with wide eyes.

"It's weird, right? My best guess is she took them up until I was born."

Ember peeled back the plastic of one of the pages. With care, she removed the photo of the cars and flipped it over. "Nineteen seventy-five. You guessed right."

"The cars and the pictures of Dad are in the back." She turned the pages to show Ember.

"Did you ever see him looking like this?"

"Young?"

"At peace." Ember ran a finger over the photo, then returned the photo of the car to its spot.

"I don't think so. That was how Mom saw him."

"Must've been nice." Ember closed the book.

"I know. We didn't see that side of him."

"Never. What does this all mean?" Ember said.

"It means that Mom had a life once and she gave up that life to raise a family. She spent all her years taking care of us and not herself. Did she regret it? Did she wish for even one second that she had made different choices? Was she lost?" Tears stung the back of her eyes. She turned her face away from Ember and watched the sun's rays streamed through the clouds.

She had been lost. She too had a life filled with choices to take care of someone else.

"You're not Mom." Ember took her hand.

"Really? I think we're more alike than I want to admit. I don't want to find myself looking at the end of my life and thinking I never did one thing for myself."

"You left Frank. That was big."

"It's not enough. I don't want to settle anymore. You know what, if Paige doesn't want to go to college, then so be it. I'm going to take care of myself from now on." Her heart pounded with the declaration as if she and Ember had gone for that run. She meant every word.

"Good for you. You deserve it."

"I was thinking about dropping that cooking class. It's going horribly. But I'm going to stick it out." She would finish the class because she had wanted to. After that, she would figure out her next step. She didn't need Mav.

"Is it the class or is it Mav?"

"It's both." She filled Ember in on the latest developments. "He needs to figure out what he wants too. I don't think he knows any better than I did."

"Maybe you two can figure it out together."

"I doubt it. He's dealing with something from his past. A divorce maybe. I know he lost his restaurant, but I don't know why." She hadn't searched the internet to find out. Deep down she didn't want to know unless he wanted to share it with her. And if it was too hard for him to speak about, then it would always be between them. His past would always chase him.

"Ask him."

"I implied I had an idea. He denied it."

"That's not asking," Ember said.

"Why are you pushing so hard for him? He could be the worst person for me."

"Petra, every time you say his name your face beams. You could light up a stadium. He's under your skin. You won't be able to shake him. Trust me. I know." Ember pointed to the side of the house.

Raf sauntered toward them. His black hair stuck up in different directions. But his gaze landed on Ember and his brilliant smile blinded her. Ember ran into his arms. Raf picked her up and swung her around. He said something Petra couldn't hear, and Ember laughed.

Petra's heart squeezed. She wanted that closeness. That connection that made the whole world fade away. She wanted the man who supported her dreams and understood her needs. She wasn't sure if Mav was that man for her, but God help her, when she saw him, nothing else mattered. And she believed she could face anything with him. He had been the only person who calmed her fear of storms.

"I have to go." She stood and wiped the back of her pants. A raindrop fell on her.

Ember and Raf were lost in each other and didn't notice her retreat.

Petra was happy for her sister. But when she pulled the car out of the driveway and headed for home, the Bon Jovi love ballad on the radio made her cry.

CHAPTER SEVENTEEN

Petra dragged herself onto the front porch and dropped into the rocking chair. The spindles dug into her sore back and the weathered wood pulled at her leggings, but she was too tired to worry about the state of her clothing.

After leaving Ember's, Petra had come home and tore the basement apart again, looking for more photos or an explanation as to why her mother had completely stopped taking such pretty photos. She had hoped to stumble upon a diary even. But all she found was over forty years of items saved with the promise that someday they might find their use again. Her parents had kept everything— every useless, worthless thing.

The night was sticky, but a warm breeze pushed the hair off her face. The day hadn't cooled much, but the house was hotter. She had no desire to be inside.

She sipped at the cold iced tea and pressed her damp fingers against her cheeks. She'd try again tomorrow to find another clue to her mother's past when she was fresher and not frazzled by the unexpected photos and by her fight with Paige.

She had tapped on Paige's door before she had ransacked the basement. Paige had been sprawled on her stomach, binge-watching a series. "I'm sorry about fighting with you," she had said.

Paige had paused the show and met her gaze. "Thank you for saying that. Did you eat dinner?"

She hadn't known if she should be relieved that she and Paige had hit a quiet impasse or furious that her daughter was ready to move on to the next thing she needed. But in the end, she had whipped up a quick dinner of grilled chicken flat breads. Paige had seemed appreciative as she dug in and ate every bite. She had even helped clean up before she hopped in the car and went to visit Junior.

Now, Petra relished in the solitude and the night songs of the cicadas. Candlewood Falls definitely had its perks. And space was one of them. She let out a heavy sigh and sunk further into the chair. Maybe it wasn't so uncomfortable after all. She could get used to spending quiet nights alone on this porch.

A car turned into the driveway, two beams of light bouncing up and down as the vehicle made its way toward her.

"So much for alone time," she said to herself. But she wasn't expecting anyone unless it was Ember who could never sit still and had decided a drop-in was better than a call. It didn't matter that she had just been with Ember.

The car parked, and the engine quieted, but the headlights remained on, blinding her. She put up a hand to ward off the glare. The car door opened with a loud creak and groan as if the door had swung one too many times.

"Petra, is that you?" Mav's deep voice carried across the way to her. The headlights went out, but bright spots danced in front of her eyes, breaking the image of Mav into several pieces.

"What are you doing here?" She must look a fright. Her hair was a mess. She ran a hand through it, tugging into place. She wore her *work in the dirt* clothes. A little warning that he was coming over would have been nice.

"I hope it's not too late." He stood by the car. Enough light from the porch cast its glow over his muscular frame. The man was unfairly handsome.

"That doesn't answer my question. Did you come here to continue our earlier argument?"

"Wow. No. I came to say I'm sorry. Wait—" He opened the car door and leaned in. "I brought a bottle of wine from the local winery as a peace offering. River's Edge I think it's called." He held up the bottle for her to see. The gesture may be nice and she might even enjoy him trying to be humble if she wasn't still furious with him for being so pigheaded.

"It's called the River Winery. It's been owned by the River family for a long time. A lot of crazy stories with that lot." She had heard most of them from her mother who had spent time with the winery's matriarch, Weezer. Petra's heart crimped for a second. Missing her mother snuck up on her and stole her breath.

"You'll have to tell me a few some time." Mav closed the space between them and stood on the bottom step. He looked up at her through his long lashes. The crinkles around his eyes when he smiled in that impish way sent a warm flush down her spine.

"Stick around long enough, you'll hear them whether you want to or not." Weezer River was a bit of a legend in town with her beauty parlor-styled hair and her overalls stuffed into combat boots. Weezer and her husband Carter had seven children, all of whom had left town at one time or another for various and suspicious reasons. Though some had returned. Even now, the youngest daughter, Zinfandel, was kicking up another scandal.

"So, small-town syndrome is a real thing," he said.

"Are you sticking around?" She clamped her mouth shut, but it was far too late. The question hung between them as thick as orange marmalade on a biscuit.

"At least until the end of the class. Oh, I forgot something else." He ran back to the car, this time pulling open the back door and returning with a white bakery bag. "I saw this at the grocery store. It looked pretty good considering not all grocery bakeries are the best. I thought we could share it. If you want that is. You never said if you wanted me to stay. You want me to stay, right?" His wide eyes were full of expectancy. She bit her lip to keep from giggling.

"Depends on what you brought." Her curiosity was piqued. He'd shown up here unannounced and was trying to win her over with wine and sweets. The least she could do was give the guy a chance.

"A fruit tart." He pulled it out of the bag. The tart was covered in blueberries, raspberries, and blackberries that glistened from the glaze brushed over it. The crust looked fresh and dense. Her stomach growled and betrayed her.

"Come inside. I'll get us some dishes and wineglasses." She turned, but didn't wait for him. He'd have to keep up.

But he was right on her heels, maybe nervous like her, maybe confident. His spicy scent made her forget her senses for a second. She nearly turned around and planted a kiss on him. Oh, Ember would have a field day with that one.

"How is the packing going?" He slid onto the stool by the counter as if he'd done it a thousand times. He fit in the dated kitchen like a favorite sweatshirt washed to the perfect softness, something she could wrap inside and get comfortable with.

"Not great. I keep allowing myself to get distracted." Like now, she wanted to say. But in a good way.

"So, you don't live here permanently?"

A tiny bubble of laughter slipped over her lips. "I don't live with my parents, if that's what you're trying to ask me. Though my daughter will be back eventually. She's at a friend's house."

She cut the tart and slid the plate toward him. He came around the counter and took the bottle opener from her hands. His touch was warm, gentle. His hand covered hers completely. A magnetic pull grabbed her from her center and drew her closer to him.

"I can help you with the wine." His voice dropped into a gravelly rumble. He popped the cork with ease and poured for them. "Where do you live, then?"

She held his steamy gaze over the rim of the glass. "Here temporarily. Until I figure out my next move." The wine was a dry rose that paired nicely with berries. He had thought this visit through. Her insides hummed. He would think of everything. That was his job as a chef.

"Relocating just like me."

"It looks that way. But I think Candlewood Falls is my stop for now. I don't want to start over in a new town. I have family here."

"And it's familiar." He poked at the fruit with his fork. He hadn't touched the wine.

"That too. Do you like living here?" She popped a berry in her mouth and savored the burst of sugar on her tongue. She had built up an appetite from working in the basement or maybe all her senses were on high alert because of Mav and that was why everything tasted so good.

"Truthfully, I don't know. There's a lot of nice things here, but I'm not sure if it's for me just yet." He held his tart-filled fork out for her. "Taste this custard. This is almost homemade."

She hesitated.

"I don't have germs. I promise." His devilish smile and playful arch of his brow pushed her over the edge.

She dragged her lips down the fork tines with slow deliberation. If he was going to taunt her with suggestions, she would taunt back. Flirting was kind of fun. "What will help you decide to stay?"

He cleared his throat and took a sip of wine. "I was hoping you."

"Me?"

"What do you really think of our cooking class?"

Her opinion of his class was the way to help him decide? She didn't quite understand. "It's not what I expected. I thought we would show up each day and you would teach us something we could build on and by the end we'd make a great meal and have some skills. But you aren't what I expected either."

She had expected someone who was more like some of the chefs on the cooking channels. Either a little goofy with a round boy face or a stickler for rules and details with frown lines so deep a truck could drive through them. But he was neither of these things. He was quiet until he wasn't. He knew what he wanted, but only said it in bursts and flames.

"I'm not sure I want you to elaborate on your opinion of me." He returned to the tart, but pushed the fruit around on the plate instead of eating it.

"I've never had a teacher who doesn't want to teach." She had gone too far by making mention of their fight earlier and ruined all the flirting like forgetting a casserole in the oven. He would be running for the door in seconds.

"I don't want to teach. I'm not even sure I want to cook." He pushed the plate away.

She also hadn't expected such an honest answer. "Then why do it?"

"I have reasons. I think they're the right ones, but they might not be enough."

"When is the right reason ever not enough?"

He turned the wineglass in his hand. "Is it wrong to want to be inspired again? I want to remember the feeling of accomplishment. Watching someone's face when they tasted my food was an adrenaline high like no other. But since my wife died, I'm stuck."

So, that was the reason for his struggle with being a chef. It had something to do with a fractured heart.

"You must've loved her a lot." Her heart broke for this man who was so grief-stricken he had lost his desire to move forward. Her divorce had derailed her, even though she had wanted it, but the two griefs were not the same.

"I did love her, but our marriage wasn't perfect. We fought all the time because I spent long hours at the restaurant. She hated that. She wanted me to give up my dream for her. We had a fight the night she died too. That's why I don't cook anymore. It isn't fair."

"Wouldn't she want you to be happy?"

"Not at the restaurant." He smirked. "I'm sorry. I didn't come here to talk about my past and put a damper on the evening. Really, I didn't."

"It's fine. I'm glad you shared it." Now she knew where she stood with this man. She couldn't compete with a ghost. And she didn't want to try.

"My brother offered me a chance to be head chef again."

"That's great." The wine turned sour in her mouth. The first man she had found attractive in ages was still feeling guilty about his wife's death and wasn't even going to stick around town for very long. She really needed to be more like Ember. Ember wouldn't have hesitated to kiss Mav and find out what was under those clothes. Petra had waited too long and missed her opportunity because now she knew too much.

"Hey, are you still with me?" Mav took a step closer.

"I'm sorry. What were you saying?"

"I said I won't leave teaching until our class is over. If I take the job, that is. I haven't decided. Can I take you tomorrow to see the spot they're considering? And I'd like to hear what you think about some of the farms in town."

"Where is this place?"

"Bash mentioned a possible place in Candlewood Falls

and he texted me another spot that's about an hour away in Jersey City. Tomorrow we'd see the place in town."

"You want me to help you decide to leave." She had no right to him, couldn't compete with the memory of his wife even, but she didn't want him running out the door just yet, and if he took a job in Jersey City, she would never see him again. The class would be over soon.

Things were moving quickly, but she needed more time to think.

"Or stay, Petra. You can convince me to stay too."

"How exactly am I supposed to do that?"

"Like this." He leaned in to kiss her. His lips were soft against hers. She closed her eyes and forced all the practical thoughts away. She could be practical later when she was alone. For now, she would enjoy the touch of his hands on her back.

He tangled his fingers in her hair and tugged her head back, taking the kiss deeper. His tongue found hers, diving and swirling until she thought she wouldn't be able to breathe. But she was hungry for more of him and kept the kiss going. All the while, her hands explored the contours of his strong and solid chest.

She had wanted to touch him from their first kiss. The reward had been worth the wait. She ran her thumbs under his t-shirt right above the top of his shorts. The hair around his navel was a soft fuzz, teasing her to find out what else was under that shirt or below his shorts. The room heated up or maybe it was her boiling over. Sweat prickled the back of her neck.

Kissing had never made her body quake, but now she was certain her knees would give out and they'd fall to the floor in a confusion of arms and legs. Her body ached, wanting his expert hands all over her, inside her. What would it be like to take him upstairs and undress him slowly, watching him as she removed each piece of clothing until he was naked in her bed? Hard. Strong.

The feverish thoughts confused her logical side. She couldn't take him upstairs tonight. Paige would be home soon and how would she explain the new man coming out of her room?

He moved his hands without hesitation and ran them over her abdomen, stopping inside the waistband of her cotton shorts. He moved one hand to her back and cupped her breast through her bra with his other hand, stroking her nipple. A moan floated deep in her throat. Tonight moved like a spinning ride at an amusement park. She wanted to get off, but she wanted the ride to keep going more. Being dizzy had never felt so good.

Their bodies swayed as if a love song crooned in the background, guiding them. His hands were all over, igniting every inch of her. She tangled her fingers into his long hair and tugged, taking the kiss deeper this time. His arousal pressed against her as her reward. She had the power to do that to the man. Which only made her want the ride with him even more.

The loud voice in her head put on the brakes. *Don't jump without looking. This isn't you.* She eased out of the kiss, gripping his waist with her fingertips. "Um... I like this a lot—"

"But it's going too fast." He ran his thumb over her bottom lip.

"A little. I haven't been with another man besides my husband in over twenty years. I don't know how to do this with someone else." Always the safe one. She could almost hear her sister saying it.

"You were doing just fine. Trust me." He placed a small kiss on her lips.

"I just need to slow down a bit." She berated herself for being foolish. She was a grown woman who could do what she wanted with her body. If she wanted to sleep with a man she hardly knew, so what? Who was going to stop her? Besides herself? Still, she hesitated. Consequences followed actions. She didn't want to make a mistake she couldn't undo.

"Whatever you want." He nibbled by her ear and wrapped his arms around her, holding her close.

She wanted more of his lips over her body, leaving marks of arousal on every spot, marking her, searing her. She wanted to rip his clothes off and have sex on the kitchen table, but not tonight. She took his chin between her two fingers and turned his gaze to hers.

"Mav, I don't understand my feelings for you completely."

He took two steps back. Their connection floated away like tendrils of smoke leaving the fire. "Then we wait."

"I know I'm sending mixed signals. I don't know if I want to wait, but I don't know that we should... you know... get it on." She squeezed her eyes shut.

He placed a soft hand on her cheek. "Hey, look at me."

She did as he asked.

"Come with me tomorrow to see this restaurant spot. Afterward, let me make you dinner, if you don't mind coming to my tiny apartment. We can try again then, if you're comfortable. And if all you want to do is make out, I'm game for that too."

"After class then?" He made it so easy for her. He seemed to understand her in a way Frank had never been able to.

"Right after class we'll go. And maybe you can give me a tour of your family's orchard. I'd like to see that."

"Thank you for understanding. And of course, I'll bring you to the orchard. I haven't been there since I've been back."

"Do you want me to leave now?"

"No." She wanted to go back to kissing, but he was right about tomorrow. They could take their time, get to know each other a little better.

He handed her the wineglass. "Do you want to finish the tart?"

"I want you to try the food I made tonight. I thought we could cook it in class tomorrow." She opened the fridge.

"We aren't using your recipe." His voice turned cold and sliced through her. Her hand stopped midair.

"Why not?"

"Petra, I realize I didn't handle things in class well today, but I don't need you undercutting me. I can't have you becoming the teacher." His brows creased.

"Well, you said you didn't want to be a teacher. You walked out on Titi this morning because you were so frustrated with her."

"Just because I don't want to teach doesn't mean I won't do it. I have the recipes planned for this food truck competition. We need to practice them and only them so we can win."

"We can't win if we don't work together." And that was something he hadn't bothered to teach them. In fact, they hadn't learned much at all. At least with her simple recipe, and the fact she had a ton of practice juggling the emotions of a teenager, she could coddle Titi and Niko into performing at least at some level.

"Then the three of you will have to learn how."

"By you teaching us." Which brought them right back to where they had started. He didn't want to teach, and he didn't want any help from her. Or probably from anybody, if she had to guess.

"No, by you not trying to be in charge of everything."

"I don't have to be in charge of everything." But Frank had accused her of the very same thing. That was why he claimed he didn't share the financial problems of the business with her. She would have swooped in and tried to take over. He had wanted to feel like a man and not have his wife save him. But because he had been so stubborn, they had lost everything. Mav could make them lose everything too. She needed to win the competition just to feel as if she had accomplished something. And not end up like her mother.

"You just admitted to having a recipe to teach the class. I know you don't have a lot of faith in me, right now. After all, I am the guy who can't be counted on, but this is my class and my project. And I will not let you down, Shelby."

"Excuse me?"

He blanched. "I mean, Petra. You know what I meant."

"No, in fact, I don't know what you mean. But I do think it's time for you to go." She went to the door on shaking legs. No man had ever called her another woman's name. He was still in love with his late wife. He just didn't see it.

Mav shoved his hands in his pockets and hung his head. "I'm sorry," he said, passing her in the hallway and letting himself out.

Part of her wanted him to stay, to fight for her. She might've caved. But the other part no longer wished to be a consolation prize. She tossed the tart into the garbage and poured the wine down the drain. She scrubbed the counter clean before crumpling into the kitchen chair. She wanted all signs of him gone.

The clock above the window ticked into the full silence of the house. This place was not the noisy home of her childhood where kids yelled from all corners, the television blasted to be heard above the clatter of dishes and pans.

The house had always smelled of warm food and comfort. Her mother had made this place a home in spite of the cold water that ran through her father's veins. Now, she was alone, and the emptiness strangled her. She didn't want to spend years of her life by herself. But she would always be if she continued to expect too much of others.

She wasn't being fair to Mav. He had suffered a terrible loss and still carried the weight of it on his back. Had no one told him his wife's death wasn't his fault? Not that she wanted to minimize the loss. That would be disrespectful and hurtful.

She was grieving the loss of her mother, but unlike Mav's wife, Mom's time had come. The difference was Mom had the power to decide. Mom had taken control. Mav must feel helpless. And she had only added to that by allowing hurt feelings to throw him out the door.

She did like planning and taking care of things. She was the oldest and a mom. She only wanted to protect the people she cared about, and she cared about her two class-mates. She liked them more each day. That was why she had found the recipe.

She needed to learn to let go and let other people have their breathing space. Like Ember and her sister Nyx. Nyx was the expert in giving someone their space by staying away from all of them.

No matter how hard she tried to hold on, she would not be able to stop bad things from happening. Not to Paige or her mom or Mav. She should've been a safe place for him to lean.

She jotted a quick text to Paige, telling her she'd be back later, grabbed her keys, and headed out the door.

CHAPTER EIGHTEEN

Mav parked alongside Bash's car near the garage apartment. His gut was twisted into a pretzel knot and not the good kind with spicy brown mustard. He had acted like a jerk around Petra, and how stupid could he have been for calling her Shelby? At least they weren't in bed. He didn't even want to think about that kind of mistake.

Not that he would call Petra by his late wife's name while making love. He and Shelby never had the name-shouting kind of sex. Things in the bedroom were okay, but it wasn't knocking off the proverbial socks. Maybe that had been part of their problem. The intimacy wasn't there. He had preferred his affair with his restaurant. He was in charge in that kitchen and his mistress had no expectations of him, accepted him moods and all. *In charge.*

Exactly what he had accused Petra of. If she never spoke with him again, he would understand. He was the biggest control freak he knew. But when she gnawed on the corner of her lip while she was working out a recipe, all he wanted to do was kiss that spot and tell her how amazing she was. Why hadn't he done that instead of calling her the wrong name and getting mad because she had stepped up where he had failed?

"No wonder why you don't ever get laid," he said under his breath.

A car turned into the driveway, its tires crunching against the gravel. Clark's car was in its usual spot, so it wasn't his landlord returning home. Maybe Bash met a lady at the local bar, Murphy's or some name like that, and she was coming over for a nightcap. He loved having his brother around, but if they were going to make this a permanent thing, they would need to find another place.

The car parked and the headlights extinguished. The car door flew open. "Mav?"

Definitely not for Bash. His heart swelled and cut off his air. He couldn't speak. His luck may have changed. Petra hurried over to him.

"I'm so sorry." Her hands fluttered around her face. "I should not have thrown you out. I should not have gotten mad when you called me Shelby. It was childish and immature. I know you miss your wife. It must be very hard for you without her."

He took her hands in his and held them against his chest, hoping his heart would slow down and he could breathe. "You have nothing to be sorry for. It's me. I haven't been with a woman who has shoved me off-balance in a very long time. Truthfully, Shelby and I weren't one of those soulmate kind of couples. Or whatever you want to call us. We cared about each other, even loved each other, but there was so much missing in our relationship."

"You don't have to explain." She looked up at him with hurt in her beautiful blue eyes. Hurt he put there.

"I do. I need you to know that calling you Shelby was some kind of misfire in my brain. She always got mad at me for being me. For a split second, I heard her, but I know in my soul you aren't her. You're nothing like her." He didn't know how to make her understand.

"How can you know so much about me?"

"I know I never felt in all my years of marriage with Shelby the way I feel in this short time with you. You... you..." The right words to explain how she sent him reeling all the time stayed out of reach. He would have to show her, instead.

He leaned in and placed a small kiss on her lips, giving her an easy out if she wanted one. No tongue, no pushing her lips apart. He braced for the slap across his face, but when she kissed him back, he swung for a home run.

The taste of wine was still on her. He could stand in his driveway and savor her all night. He wanted to memorize every curve, to drizzle honey over her breasts, to call out her name as their bodies shook with unadulterated satisfaction.

She held his face with her soft, small hands and kissed him deeply. She barely came up to his chin. He loved her petite size and wanted to keep her safe. Though he wasn't sure if he could. He didn't want to mess things up with her. She deserved the best of everything and he might not be the man to give it. Starting something with her could be fatal for him. And it would hurt her too if things didn't work out. He had no plans to stay. She wanted to make this town her home. She didn't need him. And that was a good thing at the end of the day.

He eased out of the kiss. "Petra, I really like you, but if we're going too fast, just say it. I don't want you to regret being with me." He wouldn't be able to live with himself. The pain of hurting two women he cared about would crush him. Losing Shelby nearly had. It would take very little to set him on that path again.

"Yesterday, even earlier today, I would've wanted to plan out every detail of our first time together. I don't have to do that. I can let things happen. At least I can try." She ran her hands over the front of his chest, frying out his brain.

"I should've said this sooner. I don't have any condoms with me. I didn't anticipate falling for a woman while I was here." He hadn't had sex in months. He wasn't into meaningless flings which meant he hardly had sex anymore. Sad but true. And since he hadn't been interested in anyone recently, there hadn't been a reason to even carry a condom.

She offered him a shy smile. "That's okay. I have them."

"You do? I mean... I know you like to be prepared, but..."

"My sister gave me some. She shoved them in my purse in case, you know, something happened between us." She twisted his shirt in her fists.

"You told her about me?"

"A little. She encouraged me to sleep with you." She looked up at him through her lashes.

"I will have to remember to thank her."

"Oh, please don't. I'll never hear the end of how she

was right. She's always trying to get me to be more spontaneous like her. It always works out for her. She slept with her boyfriend on like the second date and now they're madly in love and planning a family." She rolled her eyes.

"I take it you don't like him." He pulled her closer to him, wanting to feel every part of their bodies connect.

"No, that's not it. I like Raf. He's a good guy. It's just... never mind. We can talk about my family dynamics another time. I don't want to ruin the mood."

"Not possible." He would always want to make love to her. It wasn't just her appearance or the way the moonlight cast a mystical glow over her. She was special. She demanded the best of him. He was attracted to the way she tried to shape and arrange all the food she was cooking to be exactly the way she wanted when all she had to do was let go and let nature takes it course.

"Can we go inside?" She tilted her head in the direction of his place.

"Would you mind waiting out here for just a second? I wasn't expecting you, and I want to clean up a bit."

"I don't care what your apartment looks like as long as there's a bed or a couch even."

"Please, let me make it a little nicer." He would rather take her to a grand hotel and make love to her on a king-size bed with soft music playing and roses on the side table. He would open a good bottle of wine and feed her warm brie with sugar-kissed cranberries while she was naked. Next time he would do all that. But tonight he had to do one thing first.

"Okay. I see it means a lot to you. I'll wait right here." She tucked her hair behind her ear.

He ran up the apartment steps two at a time and threw the door open. Bash lay sprawled across the sofa in basketball shorts and no shirt. He watched something on his tablet, but glanced up when Mav barged in.

"I need you to get out of here. Right now." He waved toward the door. "And don't ask any questions. Don't say one word. Just get in your car and come back either in the middle of the night or tomorrow."

Bash pushed up with a languid motion. One eyebrow arched. "Does this have something to do with the pretty lady in the driveway?"

"Just put on a shirt and go. And don't say one word to her on the way out either. Well, you can say hello because I don't want her to think you're a rude asshole, but no charming her. And how did you know she was here?"

"For one, I looked out the window when your car pulled up and then again when the second car pulled in. For another, I'm pretty sure there aren't two women you want to take to bed in this town, and by the way you're throwing my shirt at me and demanding I leave my home, I'm guessing you have a chance to get lucky." Bash smirked, probably enjoying every second of how uncomfortable he was making Mav feel.

Bash shoved his feet into his sneakers. "We're going to need to get a bigger place," Bash said. "And don't do it on the couch since I have to sleep here later."

He hadn't thought of that. Definitely not the couch. "Maybe you need your own place."

"I like living with you."

"Just get out."

Bash gave a wave and trotted out the door. Mav took a quick look from the front window. The light in the living room made it difficult to see. He turned off the lamp and went back to the window. Bash shook Petra's hand.

The blood burned in his veins. His brother never listened to anyone but himself. He wasn't worried Bash would try to make a move on her. He would never do that. But Bash would say embarrassing things about him and he didn't want Petra believing his little brother's remarks.

Instead of running outside and smacking Bash in the head, he quickly made the bed and tossed his clothes onto the floor in the closet. It wasn't exactly perfect, but maybe in the dark, she wouldn't notice.

He hurried back outside. She waited for him at the bottom of the steps. The porch light cast her in a warm glow. She worked her bottom lip under her teeth.

"You are beautiful." He stood opposite her, taking her hand.

"Thank you. I'm a little dusty from being in the basement."

"Do you want to take a shower?"

Her eyebrows shot into her hairline.

He held his hands up to show he meant no harm. "Not that you need to or have to. I mean if it would make you more comfortable or... relax or... Wow. I'm really screwing this up, aren't I?" He wanted to yank his tongue out of his mouth and replace it with a better, cooler model.

"Right now, I want to go inside." Still holding his hand, she climbed the steps.

"I'll follow you, then."

≈

Petra was too nervous to pay much attention to the details of Mav's apartment. They had crossed the living space in two steps so it was cozy. The bedroom wasn't much bigger. The bed took up most of the room. He drew the curtains almost shut, letting in a sliver of moonlight. Just enough to keep her from banging her shins on the bed or dresser. She hoped they wouldn't be doing much standing anyway. They would be plenty fine on the bed together.

But her nerves bounced around in her belly like angry birds. What if he didn't like it? She had never thought of herself as a sexual person. She had enjoyed sex most of the time during her marriage, but did all men enjoy the same things?

Mav pulled out his phone and tapped at the screen until a melodic bluesy song filled the awkward silence. He drew her into his arms and swayed with her like they did in her kitchen.

"I like to dance," he said. "I'm not very good at it, but the swaying and the touching can be erotic."

Their hips rocked side to side. He spun her around so her back was to his front. His arms circled around her waist, holding her close as they moved together to the music. He rested his chin on her shoulder and sang the words to the song in a low whisper. She pressed against him, his hard muscles supporting her.

His lips found her neck while his hands explored her abdomen. She entwined her fingers with his when he dragged his hands over her thighs. His touch made her crazy. His hands were the hands of an expert. He created with those hands. And she wanted them touching her everywhere.

She turned in his arms to kiss him again. "I want to get lost with you."

Their mouths met. She had waited her whole life for a man's kiss to reverberate through her body the way Mav's kisses did. She wasn't sure how she was even standing anymore.

He scooped her up as if she weighed nothing and deposited her on the bed. He pulled his shirt over his head and slid beside her. "Are you comfortable?" he said.

"Very." She could not think of another place she wanted to be. The mattress cradled her, and Mav's lips found her neck, then dipped to her collarbone.

"If I had been prepared for this, I would have seduced you with food until you begged me for more." He drew circles with his tongue, teasing, taunting.

"It looks like you don't need the food." She arched her hips to help him pull her shorts off. But if she had been prepared, she would've worn her black dress that accented her shape and made her boobs look great. But she would've left her panties at home. She would've put on a little makeup and maybe some perfume. She would've let him feed her until the ache between her legs was unbearable. Much like it was now. No, he did not need the food.

Their hands pushed and pulled their clothes until there was nothing between them and their bodies were free for exploring. She ran her tongue down the center of his chest. He gripped her shoulders when she lingered on his delicious hip bone.

"Petra, that feels amazing, but I want this to last. You keep that up, and we'll be over before we start."

With only a pinch of regret, she slid up, his soft chest

hair tickling her, and brought her lips to his again. She enjoyed the way he gripped her bottom.

He rolled them until he was on top of her, gripping her wrists and holding her hands over her head while he explored each breast with his tongue, then nipped them with his teeth. His bristly stubble scraped at her sensitive skin. The tantalizing pain mixed with pleasure in the perfect pairing.

She gripped his hair as his mouth destroyed her in the best way possible. His hands moved over her hips and ran back up again. She reached for him, wanting to learn the full length of him. He groaned and kissed her hard.

"Mav?"

"Hmm?" He looked at her with hooded eyes.

"I'm not trying to rush this, but the condom is in my purse."

"Okay."

"In the car." The reality of their predicament was cold water on the fire. She sat up. "I'll get it."

"Absolutely not. You stay naked in my bed. I'll grab your purse." He shoved his legs into his shorts, his erection straining against the fabric. Another warm glow fell over her. She made the sexiest man she had ever been with want to run out to her car with his arousal in plain sight.

She lay back on the pillows that smelled spicy like him. She closed her eyes and focused on the pulsing need coming from her core and ran her fingertips up her torso.

"Wow," he said, standing in the doorway, out of breath. "You are the sexiest woman I have ever been with."

Heat flushed her cheeks. She didn't know what to say.

"You make me feel good." She tried, but couldn't meet his gaze.

He undressed and climbed back into bed with her. "Petra, please look at me." His voice was a whisper. "I have never felt this good with anyone." He kissed her again.

They touched and kissed until she was sure she would shatter into a million pieces. His hand slipped between her legs, finding the place that needed him most. The longing was an ache so strong that when he touched her, she nearly exploded then and there. He coaxed her closer and closer to oblivion, but pulled back each time before she could fall off the edge.

She paused them just long enough to dig around in her purse for what they needed, then returned to the warmth of his arms. He slid on the condom and positioned himself between her legs.

"Are you ready?" He gave her a devilish grin.

She was more than ready, but her words failed her. She was too focused on the tip of him at her entrance. She nodded and guided him inside her.

He moved slowly at first, and she wrapped her legs around his waist to give him more room, taking all of him in. She cupped his face so she could look into his beautiful gray eyes. His hair tickled her face, and she pushed it behind his ears.

His sweet, slow smile did her in. She was falling for this amazing man who had come back from a terrible tragedy, whether he knew it or not, and opened himself up to her. She admired his bravery, his determination to do things his way. Her heart swelled, matching the waves of desire their rhythm created.

She raised her hips to meet his, the tension inside her twisting and turning until she could no longer stand it. She gripped his back and let go of her control. Her body was racked with spasms that brought tears to her eyes. Tears of relief and joy. Not sadness.

With a final thrust, he buried his face in her neck and gripped her bottom. When he was complete, he rested his forehead on hers. Their bodies slick with sweat.

"Petra," was all he said.

And it was all she needed to hear.

CHAPTER NINETEEN

P etra hadn't heard one direction Mav gave the class. She had been too busy thinking about the night before in his bed. Whenever he walked past her station, her gaze drifted to his butt. He had a perfect backside, toned with a birthmark on the left cheek. She had nipped at it the second time they made love.

"You're smiling like the Cheshire cat with an extraordinary secret." Titi snapped a dish towel in her direction. "What gives?"

"Just enjoying class today. How are your sausage and peppers coming?"

Last night she and Mav discussed food options for the class that might be easier to grasp than some of his other ideas. Together, they had come up with using a Jersey shore style menu. It was summer, and most people equated summer with the beach and summer type food. Not that cooking a good sausage and peppers on a sub roll was easy. Mav had made sure to explain to her that barbeque was a skill too. He had taken a little offense to her implication that grilling hot dogs might give them a chance at a win. He was such an arrogant chef, but he was sexy. Very, very sexy.

"I can't get the sausage right, but I think the peppers with the onions are doing okay." Titi showed her the skillet filled with droopy peppers and overcooked onions.

"How are you doing, Niko?" She leaned over Titi to get a look at Niko's work.

"I would try these." He held up a sausage with his thongs. The outside had been charred just right. The juices shined in the overhead lights.

"Let's get those on a roll with some mayo and add Petra's peppers." Mav peered over Niko's shoulder. "Great job, Niko. You'll be on sausage duty for the competition." Mav patted Niko's shoulder, and Niko beamed.

"You don't want to use mine." Titi tossed a fork into the skillet of her peppers and onions.

"I'm sorry, Titi. You overcooked the veggies. We won't win with those." Mav shrugged. "We'll take a ten-minute break to try out the food, and then we'll go on to how to grill the perfect hot dog and how much cheese is actually enough on fries."

"You'll get it next time," she said to Titi. She wished Mav had said that to Titi instead, but he was already on to the next project. He wasn't great at bolstering the confidence of an inexperienced cook.

"Mav, may I see you in the hallway?" She headed for the door without waiting for him.

He closed the door and turned to her. The hallway was empty as it always this time of day. They were the only summer class at this end of the building, and she was grateful for the quiet. Not likely anyone would interrupt them.

Mav wrapped his arms around her waist and pulled her against him. "I've been wanting to do this all morning." He nuzzled her neck.

She choked out a laugh and put her hands on his glorious chest. "Mav, I need to talk to you. This is serious."

"So is this." He nibbled her ear and ran his hands over her bottom, tucking them into her pockets.

"Maverick, someone could see us." But the laughter betrayed her. The truth was, she wanted this man's hands all over her, and she didn't care who saw it.

He eased back with a stern expression painted on his face. "Uh-oh. The use of my full name. Okay, Ms. Wilde. Serious it is."

She smoothed down her shirt to give her hands something to do besides touch him. "You need to be more supportive of Titi."

He took a step back. "Come on, Petra. I can only do so much hand-holding. She's not getting it, and we're running out of time."

"There's more to life than winning. So what if we lose? Isn't it better to build that woman up than win a contest?"

"My goal here is to get you all to win. I'm not a psychologist, babe. You and Niko will have to carry her. If this were my old kitchen, I'd have to let her go. I'm sorry, but that's the cruel reality."

"Well, you have one thing right. You're cruel."

"That's not fair. I'm doing my job. The job you wanted me to do. Now you want to critique how I do it." He ran a hand through his hair.

"Why is it so important to win?"

"Because it is."

"At all costs?"

"What do you want me to say? That I don't have a competitive streak? That I don't want to be the best? I do. Okay? If I'm going to be in the kitchen at all as a professional, then I want to be the absolute best. That's me." He pounded at his chest.

The earlier glee in her heart had been replaced with cold dread. She yanked on the door and stalked into the classroom.

Last night, she thought she knew Mav.

Today she wasn't sure what she knew at all.

Mav kicked the wall. How could she look at him with desire one second and then look at him like he was half-eaten roadkill the next? He wasn't trying to hurt anyone on purpose, but this was business, and they could not win with Titi. She was dragging the other two down. He couldn't ask her to leave the class, but he meant what he had just said. If this was his kitchen, he would have to fire her.

Petra had all the heart, and she put it into everything she did. Her cooking, her lovemaking, all of it. But that very heart would be the thing that would destroy her in this business. She would not make it as a head chef, or any chef for that matter. Sometimes hard decisions had to be made and consequences happened.

His mind went to Shelby. He never meant to make a choice between her and work that would end up taking her life. He would forever hate himself for not going home when she had asked. But she had asked him over and over to give up his dream in order to be around more. She had wanted a family, but wouldn't start one with him until he had changed careers. "Teach," she had said.

He peered through the classroom door. Petra was helping Titi with the peppers again. Niko had moved on to the hot dogs without instruction from him. Well, he *was* teaching. This career wasn't for him. Petra could see that. She could see right through him. He didn't know how to feel about any of it. He only knew he wanted that woman with him today when he went to see the property, and he wanted her back in his bed tonight. Every night.

He shot a text to Bash, asking if he was going to be home later. He hoped his brother had plans.

Two nights in a row? Bash replied.

He could imagine his brother having himself a good laugh over his sex life. If there even was one any longer. He might've ruined that with his too-honest answer. But she needed to hear it. The truth was the truth.

A noxious smell snaked under the door and into the hall. He ran into the room, now filled with smoke. Flames shot up from the skillet and maybe the burner. He couldn't tell. Niko tore open windows. Petra fanned the smoke with a dish towel, but she was too close to the fire.

"Petra, no." He lunged for her, but not in time. The towel went up. She screamed and dropped it on the floor. Titi jumped out of the way. Niko stamped it out with his sneaker.

The sprinklers released, soaking them. The loud shriek of a fire alarm along with a computerized voice announcing instructions on how to exit blared through the building. He put his hands over his ears to stop the pain in his head.

"We have to get out of here." Niko ducked, trying ineffectively to get away from the water pouring down on them and grabbed Titi by the arm, dragging her out the door.

Petra held her injured hand with the other. The skin was pink and blistering. Red blotches had formed up her neck and on her cheeks. Her hair was plastered to her head and her sunken eyes started to roll back. He caught her before she hit the floor and ran with her outside.

What had started out as a great day because his pillows smelled like Petra, was quickly turning into a crime scene. And the woman he loved was hurt.

Because of him.

CHAPTER TWENTY

"I'm fine." Petra pushed Ember away. She didn't want all the fussing. It was a simple first-degree burn. She would be okay in a day. It was her pride that might not recover.

"You could've died." Ember grabbed her wrist to examine the big white bandage the EMT wrapped around her hand.

She pulled her hand away. "Please don't be melodramatic. The dish towel caught and I dropped it. Not a big deal."

"Then why did your boyfriend have to carry you out of the building?" Ember fisted her hands on her hips. Her blue eyes had grown to the size of mixing bowls. Her brown hair, normally styled well, was angled in many directions as if she had just gotten out of bed or had her hands in it.

"Keep your voice down. We haven't labeled what we are yet." She glanced around the scene of fire trucks, police cars, and an ambulance for any sign of Mav. He was deep in conversation with a firefighter. Titi waved her hands in the air, her mouth and arms moving at rapid speed. A police officer shifted from foot to foot, taking notes. Niko sat on the curb, talking on his phone. Everyone was safe, and she was relieved.

Some of the administration had come outside, including Mav's sister-in-law. Her short blond hair was pushed back with a torturous plastic headband. The crease between her brows was deep enough to run a truck through. She wore a bland straight skirt that hit her mid-shin and flat, sensible shoes. The anger in her eyes could set the building back on fire.

"Fine. Not your boyfriend. Your teacher had to carry you out of the building. Maybe you should go to the hospital." Ember tried to grab her hand again, but she swiped it away in time.

"I don't need the hospital. A little burn cream and I'll be back to normal in a day or two. Stop fussing over me. You're acting like Mom." The words hit her like a flash of lightning. "I miss her," she said.

"Me too. I'm sorry I'm hovering. I got scared when you called and said the school was on fire and you were burned. Raf had tried to tell me to wait and he would come with me, but I had to get to you. I couldn't wait for him to leave the orchard." Ember plopped down next to her on the back of the ambulance. The fight seemed to drain out of her. "I can't lose you."

"You're not losing me. Not that easily. And it wasn't the whole school. I had said the classroom was on fire." She pushed into Ember with her shoulder and Ember pushed back.

"Does this mean your class is going to be canceled?"

"I hope not. We were just getting it together for our big competition." But not before she and Mav had another fight. She didn't want the last thing they said to each other to be in anger. She snuck another glance at him. He was still talking to the firefighter.

"Where will you cook?"

"No clue."

Mav shook hands with the firefighter and sauntered over to them. The stress of the morning had etched itself on his face. She had put some of that stress there. "Well, it looks like we can't get back into the classroom. The smoke did too much damage," he said.

She squeezed his arm. "I'm so sorry, Mav. We'll figure something out."

"How is your hand? I'm sorry. I should've asked that first." His smile slipped. She wanted to pull him into her arms and give him the support he needed, but she wasn't sure if that was what he would want after she had attacked his teaching style. He had been right about her complaining about his methods. She had been trying to control everything again.

"My hand is okay. Are you okay?"

"We're going to have to pull out of the competition. I'll make sure the school reimburses all of you for the remainder of the class."

"I might have a solution. I'm Ember, by the way. My rude sister forgot to introduce us." Ember stuck out her hand.

Mav took it. "I'm Mav Labraccio. The failed teacher."

"That's not the way I hear it. The exact opposite, in fact." Ember snickered.

"Jeez, Ember." She hid her face because it had to be

ten shades of red. "What's this solution of yours?" Better to get on safer ground before Ember really embarrassed her.

Ember pointed before Mav could say anything. A Wilde Orchards pickup bounced into the parking lot and skidded to a stop. Raf hopped out of the driver's side and her cousin Brad unfolded from the passenger side. Great, now the whole family and the whole town would know. Her father would be calling in seconds. She had better text Paige before she overheard the news from a stranger.

"Is everyone all right?" Raf jogged up to them. He wore a Wilde Orchards t-shirt and jeans. "Ember, when you didn't answer my text, I came right over." Raf kissed Ember on the cheek. Her sister beamed.

"I rode along to make sure he didn't drive into a ditch," Brad said. He was dressed much like Raf, except his clothes were covered in dirt.

"We're all good. Thanks for coming." She stood next to Mav to show her support for him. He couldn't know that was why she had done it, but it was important to her that her family understood he was not at fault. She introduced those who hadn't met yet.

"I'm glad you're here," Ember said to Raf and Brad. "The class can't continue without a kitchen. What if they used the kitchen at the orchard where you make the donuts?"

"Wait. What?" Mav said.

"She didn't discuss this with anyone," Raf said, shaking his head. "Ember, babe, maybe you should've checked with Mav and Brad first. Or me?"

Ember waved his words away. "I'm discussing it now

in front of everyone. What do you say, Brad? It's only for a couple of weeks."

"You want me to tie up my kitchen in August when people come in droves for pick your own apples and those donuts? Can't do it. I'm sorry. I'd love to help, Petra. You are family and it's partly your orchard too, but I can't allow a cooking class at the orchard this time of year. In January, sure." Brad shoved his hands in his back pockets and rocked on his heels.

"It's not a problem. I wasn't expecting you to jump in." And she wasn't, but it dawned on her that she should have a say at the orchard. Brad was right, the business was partly hers no matter how much her father blustered.

She had been the one to leave town and the family business behind. She could've stayed and fought her father's disdain for having his daughters work the orchard. Huck had wanted sons like his brothers. And she had run because being Huck's daughter often hurt. But she was also Ruby's daughter. She had some of her mother's spunk too. And maybe her mother had come to the party late, but at least Ruby had left this world on her own terms. It was high time she declared her terms too.

"I wasn't expecting you to help out either," Mav said. "I'll think of something. Petra, I'll call you. Nice to meet everyone." Mav moved over to Titi and Niko and spoke with them without another glance in her direction. She willed him to turn around and look at her, but he didn't.

"Come on, Brad. Petra's class only needs about an hour a day for a few weeks," Ember said.

"I can't do it."

"Raf, tell him," Ember said.

"Do not put me in the middle of this. Petra, I have to

side with Brad." Raf shot Ember a stern look. Ember shook her head.

"Ember, stop." Her voice vibrated in her head. She had to put her good hand to her ear to quiet the ringing. "The whole world doesn't have to bend to your wishes. But I will say this, for the first time in my entire life I wish I had a say at the orchard."

Brad blanched. She didn't wait for anyone else to respond. She followed the path Mav had taken, hoping she'd bump into him at his car.

Now that he couldn't teach the class, Mav wanted to. Did this new desire have something to do with proving to Petra that he wasn't such a bad teacher? His insides bristled every time she implied he couldn't do it. He wanted her to see the best in him. She must see something. Last night had not been his imagination. The sex had been amazing.

When he saw that towel up in flames so near her face, his heart nearly stopped. He couldn't lose her so soon after finding her. He was in trouble where she was concerned. She had snuck in and pierced his heart.

A tap on his window startled him from his thoughts. Petra smiled and the tightness in his chest eased. He hopped out of the car and grabbed her around the waist. She sunk against him.

"I needed this," she said against his chest.

"Hey, are you okay?" He eased back to meet her gaze. The color had drained from her face and her eyes were red and puffy. He hadn't noticed the pain she was in before. *Jerk.*

"I'm better now. I didn't want to let on to my sister how much my hand hurts, and then Brad and Raf showed up. I thought I had to put on a good show. But when you walked away, I knew the only place I wanted to be was with you."

"I ruined everything for the class. You were right. I'm a terrible teacher."

"You're not. Titi's carelessness isn't your fault. Don't take this on too, Mav. Not every mistake is yours. And I'm sorry about arguing with you today."

"You were right."

"No, I wasn't. I wanted to tell you how to do your job and I have no right."

"Petra, I didn't keep my kitchen safe. And now we don't have one."

"What about at my house? Why can't we practice there? I have a grill too."

"I guess we could. As long as the school doesn't yank the class. It looks like they won't be asking me to teach in the fall either. Avery shot me a text. They're rethinking the fall class. That means I have to seriously consider Bash's offer. Are you feeling up to going with me to see the possible space?"

"I think I'm going to go home. I have more packing to do and I'm going to be slower now with this hand. I know I said I would go, but I'd also like to see Paige. You know, hug my kid kind of thing. Even if she doesn't want to be hugged. I'll guilt her with my new injury."

"Sure. I understand." But he really wanted her with him. He needed her, but she never seemed to really need him. For that one brief second that she melted into him, he hoped that she would tell him how much he meant to her, but the moment was over as quickly as it had started.

"Are you free tonight? Maybe you could come over, and we can try out my kitchen."

He had some ideas of things he wanted to try in her kitchen. "I'll come by around six. I'll let Titi and Niko know where class will be tomorrow. Thank you for offering your home."

"I want us to win." She smoothed her hand over his chest. He wanted her hands all over him.

"Will you be okay if we don't?" What would it do to her if he let her down?

"Will you?"

CHAPTER TWENTY-ONE

P etra turned in circles in her mother's sewing room. She had no idea where to begin. This tiny alcove on the second floor was more than any sewing room. It was her mother's escape place. In the corner by the window was an oversized chair covered in faded blue material. The chair had been there as long as she could remember. She would often find her mother up here with a cup of tea and a book.

A white bookcase was filled with paperbacks three rows deep, all in various poses of leaning, flat on their backs, or pages out. Mom's sewing machine, a Singer that once belonged to her grandmother, was against the wall. Her mother also had baskets of material scraps and a few smaller baskets on a small table by the machine that were filled with spools of thread in every color on the spectrum. Mom even had a few knitting projects in various stages of unfinished.

But the thing that had her breath stuck in her throat

was the white teacup on the table beside the chair. Dredges of tea on the bottom had dried to the porcelain. Her mother's pink lipstick stained the rim.

She had no idea why her father insisted that all signs of Ruby be gone by the time he returned. He never came in this room. That was also evident from the crystal vase on the windowsill. Her mother had often kept fresh flowers in it. Petra would keep the vase. It was cut crystal. When the sun hit it just right, a thousand beams of light bounced off the walls and floor.

She couldn't do it. She could not pack up another thing of her mother's. Every item that found its way from its home to an anonymous box sliced her heart into tiny fragmented pieces. The pain was too much.

The doorbell rang, saving her from another second of debate. She hurried to the door and pulled it open. The burn on her hand protested when she pressed her palm to the knob. She would have to remember to use her other hand for a while.

She wasn't expecting her visitor. She would've liked a little time to get ready. But he was three hours early. "Hi, Mav."

"Hey. I know I said I would come by around six to practice tomorrow's recipes, but I couldn't wait. I didn't want to go home to my tiny apartment and dodge Bash for the next three hours. Or worse, have him tell me I was making too much noise while he was on the phone."

"I'm definitely not ready to cook, but you can come in." She moved to the side and let him pass. The color had returned to his face since the morning's fiasco, but he still looked as tired as she felt.

"I hope I wasn't interrupting anything." He stopped inside the door. His large frame took up most of the space.

"Actually, I appreciate the interruption. I'm packing up my mother's things, and I don't want to. So, thank you."

"Are your sisters helping?"

"Do you want to go into the kitchen or maybe sit out back? There's a nice breeze now and the sun isn't beating on the deck."

"Is that your way of avoiding my question?" His smile crinkled the lines around his eyes.

"Yes and no." She needed him to move because this close all she could think about was wanting to kiss him.

He laughed and ducked his head. "Fair enough. How about if I help you pack? Then I won't feel badly about showing up uninvited three hours early and empty-handed."

"You don't have to do that. Let's go to the kitchen." She took him by the shoulders and turned him around, giving him a little shove so he would keep moving.

Explaining how she felt about her mom or the stories that might be attached to the items that he would inevitably ask about, was going to be more than she could handle. She wasn't ready to share her goodbye to her mom with anyone. It was part of the reason she didn't want her sisters here. This was her farewell.

"I know how hard it can be to put away the life of someone you love. It took me a long time to gather all of Shelby's things. Her clothes hung in our closet for months. Every time I saw them, they were a comfort and a hardship at the same time." He leaned against the counter.

"I hate the idea that my mom is going to be nothing more than items sold at a garage sale. Is that what our life becomes?"

"Have a seat." He pulled out the kitchen chair. "I'm going to mix us up a snack."

"Mav—"

"Petra, for one afternoon allow someone else to help you. Now sit." He moved around the kitchen with ease, pulling out whatever she had in the refrigerator and pantry. He found her blender and helped himself to it.

"What are you making?"

"Vegan energy balls. I wasn't expecting to find dates in your fridge. These will give us the energy to go pack." He put the plate of ten speckled brown balls in front of her. He returned to the table with two glasses of iced tea.

"Thank you." She had to admit it was a treat to have someone else make something for her to eat. She couldn't remember the last time someone cooked for her even if it was as simple as these vegan balls. She took a bite. The texture was creamy with a sweet and salty taste from the almonds and the dash of salt he put in.

"Let's go back to my earlier question. Why aren't your sisters helping you?" He sat opposite her.

She couldn't meet his gaze. She licked the remains of the vegan balls off her fingers instead. "Because I asked them not to."

"Of course, you did. Why? Don't they want to be a part of this?"

"Ember does. Nyx can't get away right now. But she would too. I wanted to be the one to take on the burden. Ember has a lot of wonderful things in her life right now.

She doesn't need the stress of this. And I had nothing. My whole life fell apart. My marriage was over. We had to sell our house to pay off debt. It made the most sense for me to do it."

"Come on." He stood and held out his hand.

"Where?" She unfolded from the chair as if someone pulled a string from the top of her head.

"To wherever you were when I rang the bell. You aren't going to do one of the hardest things a person has to do by yourself." He waved her on.

"You don't have to."

"I know I don't. Where to?"

She led him upstairs to the sewing room. He took up most of this space too. She had to put her hands on his waist to scoot past him while she explained the plan. He smelled like fresh air and chocolate.

"We can start with the books. I guess. I think the library will take them." She handed him a box.

"She had a lot of books."

"Too many. How did it go earlier with your restaurant spot?" Talking about him would distract her from the uncomfortable thoughts invading her brain about her mom. "Wait. I'll keep that one." She grabbed an old paperback by M. Kate Quinn from his hands. Ms. Quinn was Mom's favorite romance author. They had met once in Woodbridge at a reader's conference. Mom talked about it for weeks.

"Well, not that great. It was an old restaurant right off Main Street near the mill. Great spot for outdoor seating. The place went under a few years back and the building has sat empty. It seemed like it would be a good fit, having a kitchen and all, but the renovations would be extensive.

Bash wants to see if there's something in another town or even county that needs less work. There's a nice spot in Sussex County that might work. He showed me the listing."

"Is that what you want?" Sussex County was easy an hour away or longer depending on where. If that was the decided upon spot, things between them would end.

"Me? I don't want to take on renos. They never go smoothly, and they always come in over budget. The budget is tight on this so no mistakes. No pipe dreams kitchens. Simple. But Candlewood Falls is a great town with a lot of tourist traffic. I don't know about the other place. Who actually goes to Sussex for anything besides the hiking and the lakes?"

"Will you keep looking if you don't like the Sussex place?"

"It's up to Bash. It's his money. We could end up in Cape May for all I know." He taped up the first box and started on the second.

"So, you're definitely going." She hoped the disappointment in her voice wasn't obvious.

"Looks that way."

They worked in silence for a while. She organized all the sewing supplies, then labeled the boxes for easy access later in case anyone wanted this stuff. Before she knew it, the room was cleaned and the only things left was the furniture, including the sewing machine and the crystal vase. She tucked that under her arm.

"I'll put this in my room. I'll be right back."

Mav waited for her in the hall. His face shined with sweat from carrying all the boxes either into the basement or on the front porch for delivery later.

"Are you hungry?" he said.

"I could eat."

"How about if we pick up the hot dogs for tomorrow and give them a try? I make a mean potato salad, but honestly, I'm exhausted from the whole day and your hand must be hurting."

She hadn't thought much about her hand. Her fingers worked fine. As long as she didn't put pressure on the burn spot, she was okay. "We could pick up some. And if you want, we could stop at the orchard and grab an apple pie."

"A real American barbeque."

"That should be our tag line for the competition."

"I like it."

"Thank you for helping me today. I wouldn't have done half of that by myself. I can't seem to make my hands do the work. I run from the room."

"You don't need to tackle every big job by yourself. I want to help you. I wish someone would've helped me."

"It's been my experience that I have to count on myself."

"You can count on me." He pulled her close.

"But you might leave town." She was getting used to having him around. She looked forward to seeing him every day and talking to him. Then he goes and shows up right when she needed someone to take the burden of packing up that room. As if her mother had sent him to her at that moment.

"Can we take it one step at a time? I'm here now. And I'll be here until the class ends. We can figure out the rest later." He cupped her face.

Her hands instinctively went under his shirt, relishing

the feel of his skin and the texture of his muscles. "Would it be okay if we ate later?" She had other things on her mind besides food.

"What were you thinking?" He leaned in with a wicked grin.

"This." She stood on her toes and kissed him.

CHAPTER TWENTY-TWO

P etra ran around her kitchen covering her counters with trays, utensils, and bowls, enough for three of them to practice with. She organized all the ingredients she and Mav purchased yesterday after their hasty lovemaking. They had barely made it out of the hallway after she had kissed him. When their lips touched, the chemistry caught fire and she had no longer cared how sweaty she was or even how sweaty he was from carrying boxes. By the time their bodies reached the desired effect, they were drenched all over again.

He had plunged inside her within seconds. It had seemed neither of them could wait. Her pants had barely hit the floor. He had only managed to yank his shirt over his head and push his jeans out of the way. He hadn't even taken off his shoes.

They had dressed quickly afterward and ran to the store for the food to cook this morning. When they had returned, Paige and Junior were in the kitchen heating up some canned soup. Mav gave her a knowing look behind

Paige's back. Had they lingered in the glow of their incredible time together—at all—they would've been caught. They laughed like crazy afterward.

The front door opened. "Petra?" Mav's deep voice vibrated through the house.

"In here." She grabbed another mug and poured some of the coffee she had just brewed.

"Hey." He stuck his head around the archway. His smile rippled all the way to her belly. "Why did you run out on me this morning? When I woke up you were gone." He took the mug she offered, but put it on the counter. "Come here." He pulled her to him and kissed her hard on the mouth.

They had ended up at his place after the dinner at hers. They had sat with Paige and her friend Junior who filled them in on all the picking antics at the orchard. Junior seemed like a nice boy. Maybe Raf was wrong about Junior. And Paige was happy when he was around. That suited Petra for now. She and Mav had decided after dinner to take a drive and leave the kids alone. Mav had asked her to stay over. And she had agreed.

"I didn't want to wake you. You were sleeping so soundly, and I had a million things to do." Like take a shower and hopefully arrange her face into something neutral so her classmates wouldn't take one look at her and know that she was enjoying amazing sex with their teacher.

"I thought you might have had some regrets."

"No regrets." And she would stick to that if he left town. She would not be the woman who asked him to stay. "Can you help me cut up the potatoes for the salad? I boiled enough for three large batches, but it will save us time if they're already prepared. Plus, I think we can have them cut up and ready to go the morning of the competition. I searched the rules online."

"I forgot to give you guys the rules." He smacked his head. "Yeah, I'm not a good teacher. I really need a new line of work. How's your hand?"

"Good enough to cut. Listen, it takes time to be good at something. I'm sure you spent years perfecting your cooking techniques before you opened your restaurant."

"If you call making dinner for me and Bash because my old man was always working, practice, then yes."

She realized she didn't know a thing about this man's past except that his wife died unexpectedly and that he had a brother. "What was your childhood like?"

He grabbed a potato and her mother's outdated chef's knife. "Oh, you don't want to be bored with the predictable no mom and less than par father story."

"That's right. You said your mom passed away. I really am sorry." She couldn't imagine not having Ruby here every day when she came home from school or all the home-cooked meals and desserts that Ruby had for them night after night. When she was a kid, she had wished she had a mother who had a career, who did something important with her life besides cooking and cleaning, but once she became a mother herself, she understood the utter importance of her mother's job and how grateful she was that Ruby and her skills in the kitchen were a necessary constant in the life of a tumultuous teenager.

"She died about fifteen years ago, not when I was a kid. When Bash and I were little, she had decided that she didn't want to be married to our dad anymore. My father had lost his job, and they were strapped for money. They had to sell their home and move into a two-bedroom apartment, and my mother was humiliated. She had married my dad for his potential to earn money. She couldn't take it, so she left him." He sliced through the potatoes with precision, making each cube the exact size.

"But what about you and your brother?" She grabbed another cutting board and positioned herself beside him. His heat rolled off him and over her. She would much rather forget about class and take this man back to bed.

"She said another man wouldn't marry her if she had two boys in tow. We needed to live with our dad until she remarried. But when she did, she never came for us. I was about seventeen and went looking for her. I found her house. It was spectacular. A sprawling two-story red brick thing."

"Did you approach her?"

"Sure did. I pounded on the door so hard I bruised my hand. But a little girl, maybe six, I don't know, answered. She stared up at me, and I couldn't look away from her. She had Bash's eyes. A woman's voice called out from the back of the house for her. The little girl said *Mommy, a man at the door.* When she came around the corner, she stopped dead."

"What did you do?"

"I turned and left." He shrugged and kept dicing.

"You didn't say anything?"

"It hit me then. She never wanted us either. And I didn't want her anymore."

"But you didn't ask her why she left?"

"Did it really matter? She had left. My dad ended up being a vice president of a car company. He had made a ton of money. Bash is just like him. Her reason for leaving had nothing to do with money. It had everything to do with us."

"Oh, Mav, that can't be true. Did you ever ask your dad about it?"

"I did. He told me when he got the job with Chrysler, he wasn't VP yet, he went to her, but it was already too late." He had a pile of cubed potatoes in front of him while she had barely made it through the first one. His story stunned her. She didn't understand how a mother could leave her children.

"I'm sorry." She gripped his arm and squeezed so he would know she was there for him.

"Don't be. It was a long time ago." He pointed to her potato pile with his knife. "You're slacking off, lady. Slicing and dicing isn't usually the head chef's job."

"This is my kitchen, buddy. I'm the head chef here."

He tilted his head back and barked out a big laugh. "You've got me there."

"Though I'd better hurry. Titi and Niko will be here soon." She checked the clock above the window.

"About that…"

"What? Did something happen?" Titi had sworn she didn't get hurt yesterday. She had refused to go the hospital or allow the EMTs to fuss over her.

"Nothing happened. Titi called me this morning. She's dropping the class."

"She can't. We need her."

Mav arched a brow.

"Okay, not exactly need her, but she's a part of our little group. And she was more excited about taking the class than either Niko or I was. You can't let her drop."

"I tried to talk her out of it. But she insists she's

holding you two back. She wants you to have a chance to win."

"If she doesn't stay, we can drop out of the competition, can't we?"

"The contest has already started advertising the competitors."

"And they're using your name." Of course they would be. He was a draw. People would come for miles to see him.

"And now that Bash has set up this business opportunity for me, I can't cause any bad press. I'm going to need the job, and honestly, because of you, I want to try and cook again."

"Me? What did I do?"

He put the knife down and took her hands in his. His gaze smoldered. "What we've been sharing these past few weeks has woken me up."

"Mav, I don't know what to say." He had woken things in her too.

"You don't have to say anything. Forget it." He returned to this task.

She gripped his arm. "Mav, this wonderful thing between us is so new for me. And our futures are so uncertain. I've never met anyone like you. Can we just get through this morning?"

"Whatever the lady wants." He placed a kiss on her cheek and cut another potato.

"What about poor Titi?" She couldn't look at Mav and see the disappointment in his face. He had expected her to declare her feelings for him. She had seen the hope in his eyes. But she had to protect herself somewhat from the moment he left her.

"I'm sorry, Petra. We have to go on without her."

"What if I talk to her?" She put down the knife and forced herself to face him. This morning needed to be about keeping Titi on their team and not their relationship. They could deal with their feelings later.

"You could try, but I don't think it will do any good."

"I have to try. Do you know where she lives?"

"Not without looking at her class records."

"I'll call her then." She went to her phone and pulled up Titi's number. Titi answered on the fifth ring.

"Hello, Petra."

"Titi, I just spoke to Mav."

"Please don't try and talk me out of it. I'm not good for you and Niko. You have a better chance of winning without me."

"But that isn't true. We want you there. You've worked hard."

"I set the classroom on fire, honey. We all have our gifts. Mine isn't cooking. I'll come and cheer you on. I promise. I have to run. Give your man a kiss for me."

"What are you talking about?"

"Petra, honey, you can't fool an old fool. I see the way the two of you look at each other. Even if you and Niko lose the competition, you've still won. Don't let that man go. Ta-ta." Titi ended the call.

She stared at the phone.

"I'm guessing she still said no." Mav's voice dragged her gaze away from the phone and the echoing of Titi's observation in her ears. She hadn't been hiding her feelings well at all, apparently.

"What are we going to do?"

"We're going to win. I'll step in and help you and

Niko. But you two will be in charge. I can't make one decision. I can't tell you what to do when the competition heats up. You'll have to take charge and run the whole show. I think you can handle that."

Could she? Sure, she had organized plenty of classroom activities where she had to tell the other moms what to do. She had been on the team that planned the school's silent auction, bossing everyone around to get the night off without a hitch. But lead Niko and Mav of all people in a cooking competition?

She wished she could talk to her mom right now. She needed to hear her mother tell her she could do it. That she believed in Petra. Her mom was always in the wings applauding the loudest.

"Mav, I don't want to lose."

"So don't."

CHAPTER TWENTY-THREE

M av hated the spot and loved it at the same time. Bash had found the perfect location for the farm-to-table restaurant. Except it was in Jersey City—over an hour from Candlewood Falls. The building was built in the early eighteen-hundreds and most of the original materials had been restored. But the best part was the rooftop access where a garden had been planted and plenty of seating for outdoor meals or drinks. More than one farmer's market was in walking distance.

"It's great, right?" Bash turned in circles with his arms wide, that triumphant smile on his arrogant face. Just like their dad.

"Yeah, it's perfect."

"Don't sound so excited about it." Bash gripped his shoulder. "You could turn this place into a gold mine. Make us a ton of money."

"But the place in Candlewood Falls had a uniqueness. Don't you think?" It had a stone patio that was tree-lined. He had pictured small wrought-iron tables with red umbrellas for the customers to sit at as the sun set behind the mill.

"Too quaint. Too small town."

"But we were talking small." Bash was right, but he wasn't ready to take on a restaurant this size. The seating capacity was too much like the place he had lost. He'd be committed to twenty-hour days, planning menus, shopping for the right amount of ingredients, running a staff sizeable enough to handle the workflow.

"The views alone from this place are worth millions. Too bad the last owner had his head up his ass. But great for us. We can come in and get this place for a steal. And there's no reno work. That other place would need to be gutted."

"I don't think gutted is the right word." It did need a lot of work. And though the view of the mill was nice, it wasn't the harbor and the lights of New York City as its backdrop. Even so, the quiet streets of Candlewood Falls and the beautiful brunette waiting for him was the all the enticement he really needed.

"Let's take a walk around the neighborhood. We'll even stop at the farmers' markets, okay?"

"I need to get back. We have one more trial run before the competition." He had promised Petra he would be there this afternoon and he was already late. She had texted him several times, reminding him to hurry.

She didn't really need him. He knew it. She hadn't asked him once to consider staying in town for her or for them. She was too happy to get into his bed, but there was never talk about anything beyond the competition. She was still trying to figure out her own life. He didn't know where he fit into that. Maybe nowhere. He'd be a fool to turn down this opportunity. It would be back to the warehouse for him, if he did. But he couldn't make his mouth say yes to Bash.

"You're letting that competition take up too much of your time. It doesn't mean anything."

"It's important to my students." And to him. He felt something like pride when he watched Niko and Petra work together. When Titi had quit, he had fought to keep her because after all his blustering about not wanting to be a teacher, he couldn't fathom the idea of losing a student. The disappointment was as rancid as sour milk.

"You never even wanted to teach that class. And we have to put in an offer on this place before someone else comes in and snags it. It won't last."

"Why do you care about getting into the restaurant business all of a sudden?" Bash had never shown an interest when he had his restaurant. He could've used a loan in the beginning, but Bash's attention had been elsewhere.

"It's a good business opportunity."

"Restaurants are hardly that. What's the real reason?"

"Fine. I want you to start living again. When my buddy came to me with his offer, I thought I could use this to save you from yourself. But all you seem to want to do is dig roots in Candlewood Falls. You've got to want more than that."

"I don't know what I want." But roots didn't seem like such a bad idea. He hadn't had any in years. Even while he was married to Shelby, he hadn't felt attached to their home. The only place where he fit had been his restaurant. But Candlewood Falls whispered to him, as if it knew he needed to be brought home.

"Isn't it time you figured out what you wanted? It's been three years of ambling around with no direction. Do you even notice you have a very beautiful woman interested in you?"

"What are you talking about? Petra? Of course, I know."

"I don't think you do. You're hovering on the edges like you always do. You don't have any idea how to commit to a relationship."

"And you do? Aren't you living with me in that crappy apartment because you and Jess broke up?" He would not stand there and take relationship advice from his brother.

"I'm living with you because you need a kick in the ass. You said so yourself, Mav. I could rent out the top floor of a nice hotel. I don't need to live with you. I wanted to so I could help you."

"I didn't ask you for help. I don't need your help. I'm doing fine. In fact, I was doing great until Avery called. Why does everyone think I need saving?" Anger rose up from his belly and shoved out words he didn't really mean. He wasn't doing great before Avery called. He was managing. And sure, he had not wanted to teach this group of misfits, but that changed.

"Don't screw this up. Take my offer and get on with your life. Or go after the woman, but do it with all your heart. You've wasted enough time."

"I need time to decide."

"I need to give the realtor an answer. Two days, Mav. That's all you get."

Petra took in her mother's sewing room. Mav and she had done a good job making space in here. But Mom's desk still needed emptying and Petra couldn't sleep. Other rooms still required her attention, like the dining room with its sideboard and large china cabinet. She hadn't touched a thing in the kitchen either. She wasn't in the mood to tackle the bigger undertakings. Not in the middle of the night, anyway. The old-style desk with its carved legs and etched edges called to her. She ran her hand over the swirls in the wood and her fingers came away with dust.

Class today with just her and Niko was a lumpy mess. She and Niko don't have a good chemistry in the kitchen and no matter how many different ways she tried to steer the lesson, Niko wanted to do things his way. Without Mav there, they had only managed to overcook the sausage and turn the skins of the hot dogs black.

Mav had arrived long after he had said he would with excuses of getting caught in traffic on the way back from Jersey City. Traffic in New Jersey was not folklore, but that little fact did nothing to ease the worry in her chest. Niko would only listen to Mav. Without Mav at the competition for any reason including traffic, they might not win.

He had asked her to come over again, but she turned down his offer. Now she regretted that choice. At least with Mav, she had a chance to get some sleep. She threw open the window. August nights could sometimes deliver a cool breeze filled with motivation and the comfort of peace. Tonight was one of those nights, and she allowed the gentle wind to dance across her skin. The air was filled with the promise of rain. She hoped it didn't rain the day of the competition.

"Better get working," she said to herself and pulled open the top drawer. If she cleared the desk, maybe she would tire enough to sleep for an hour or two.

The top drawer was filled with paperclips and skinny rubber bands. A small snow globe ornament with *Grandma* on the bottom was tucked into the corner. Paige had given that to Ruby after a holiday trip to Cape May when Paige had to have been about three. She couldn't believe Ruby still had it.

Petra scooped up the pens, forgotten buttons, and scrap papers and dumped them in the garbage. She packed up anything that her father could use in his study and labeled that box *Huck*.

The other drawers were more of the same. Her eyelids grew heavy, and she breathed a sigh of relief. Sleep might be attainable after all.

She pulled on the bottom drawer, but it stuck. She tugged harder and toppled onto her butt when the drawer gave way. She righted herself and kneeled. This drawer was different. It was a small filing cabinet style drawer filled with folders. Each folder had a label in her mother's handwriting.

The folders held past years' planners, artwork from when she and her sisters were in elementary school, and even a few random owner's manuals from gadgets long forgotten.

"Why keep all this stuff?" She hurriedly searched through the folders. All of this would need to go to recycling, except maybe the artwork.

The last folder, tucked far in the back, which she almost missed, was green and faded with no label. The folder was thick with white paper as if a printer had vomited in it. Petra pulled the folder free and sat cross-legged on the floor as she glanced at the pages.

The first page was blank. The second one had her hand hovering over it. *Cookbook by Ruby Wilde.* Cookbook? Ruby was full of surprises. First the photos, now this.

When had her mother considered writing a cookbook? Every page was filled with typed recipes and handwritten notes on the side with adjustments and thoughts on the meal. Her mother had close to a hundred pages. Even a few photos, taken in the same style as the ones in the album Paige had found.

When she got to the end, she went back and looked again. Some of the pages had dates on them and those dates went back to when Ruby was in high school all the way through two years ago when her diagnosis had come crashing down on them all.

If it wasn't the middle of the night, she would text Ember and see if she knew anything about a cookbook. That would have to wait for a reasonable hour of the day. If she woke up Ember, she would wake up Raf too most likely. Ember had to deal with her, but Raf did not.

She wanted to talk to someone about this new discovery. She debated on calling Mav, but why should he be roused from his sleep for this? It wasn't life or death.

No lives weren't at stake. But the realization hit her square between the eyes. She didn't know her mother at all. Her mother had kept so many secrets from them about all the things she had really wanted to do and be. Ruby had been a young woman once with hopes and dreams. What had she done with all them besides shove them in a drawer?

And she couldn't ask her mom why. Grief rose up and

struck her with a hard blow. She dropped the pages, and they fluttered around her legs like the petals of a white dandelion. She wanted to talk to her mom and ask all the questions she had never asked before. She wanted her mom to fill in all the holes of her memories so she could carry on her mom's stories with complete accuracy. Didn't Mom deserve that much?

Didn't everyone?

CHAPTER TWENTY-FOUR

The crowd at the orchard dwindled. Wilde Orchards had closed twenty minutes ago, but the last of the customers bagged their apples and bought their desserts. Petra watched as families tumbled into their minivans. Mav had agreed to meet her here at closing, but he was running behind. She had packed a light dinner of grilled chicken sandwiches, potato salad because they had made so much of it during class this week, and apple cider donuts for dessert.

"Hey, Petra." Raf waved and ambled over to her. He was covered in dirt, and she shook her head.

"Do you roll in the orchards?"

"Sometimes." He laughed. "Are you waiting for Brad? I think he already left, but I could call him for you if you need him."

"No, thanks. But Brad does know I'm here. I'm... well, I kind of have a date. Not with Brad." She held up her hands to show she meant no harm.

When she had asked Mav to meet her, she hadn't

called this a date. She had only wanted to spend time with him and tell him about what she had found the night before. She still hadn't told Ember and felt a little guilty keeping that secret while Raf stood before her. Now she was lying to him too, but she wanted to hear what Mav thought first.

"Here?"

"Crazy, right?" Mav had agreed immediately. She could've flown to the sun and back at that moment. So ridiculous. They had already slept together, but being out in public with him, and not in class, made what they had more real.

"I think it's great. This place and the alpaca farm are the best locations for dates."

"Yes, I heard about that date you organized for Ember this past spring. Very romantic."

"I try." He shrugged and shoved his hands in his back pockets.

"Looks like whatever you're doing is working. My sister is very happy. Thank you for that."

"She makes me happy too. I've got a few more things to do before I head out. If you need anything for this date, let me know."

"I will." But she had everything she needed.

Mav's fancy red car pulled in and parked beside hers. A nervous fist twisted her stomach like taffy. He unfolded from the front seat and walked over to her. The dark sunglasses blocked his eyes, but his smile brought plenty of heat to her center.

"I'm not late this time. I have two minutes to spare." He kissed her cheek. He smelled of leather and citrus, perfect scents to go with a powerful man. She wanted to sniff him more.

"Let's take a walk while we still have enough daylight." She grabbed the picnic basket out of the trunk.

"Do we have to be off the property by nightfall?"

"Nope. I have an in with the owner." She had arranged the evening with Brad earlier in the day. Brad had welcomed her to be on the orchard as much as she wanted. He said he wished all her sisters and even his own sister would spend more time in the family business.

"Aren't you part owner? That was your name on the sign."

"Not me. My father and his brothers. Also my two cousins because their dad passed away some years ago. That uncle left his share to his children, Sam and Lacey. The orchard has been in the family for generations. My cousin Brad is the VP of operations. My other cousins are scattered between here and California. They aren't involved with the orchard."

"Do they sell their apples to wholesalers?"

"And to local markets as well."

"Would they ever grow something besides apples?"

"They grow pumpkins."

"What about vegetables?"

"You'd have to ask Brad."

"This is a great piece of land. And it already has a distribution plan if they sell to wholesalers. I would love to have an inside connection to a place like this for a farm-to-table experience." The sun's brightness couldn't rival the glow on Mav's face. He belonged in a restaurant, making people food they loved. He had denied himself joy and his customers his wonderful food. Her heart sunk a little.

They found a spot in the middle of the pick your own field where she could spread out the blanket and food. The sun dipped into the treetops like caramel sauce. He stretched out his long legs and leaned back on his elbow. He poked a potato with a fork and fed it to her.

"I found something last night." She told him about the late-night packing and stumbling upon her mother's cook-book and the photo album.

"You could've called me."

"I didn't want to wake you. But I did want to share it with you." There hadn't been another person, besides Ember, who she had wanted to talk to about her little discovery. "My mother never went after her dreams. And I can't ask her why. What held her back? All night I kept thinking, I'm just like her. I never went after my dreams either."

"That can't be true. You're a mom. You were married. You signed up for the cooking class, hoping it would take you down a new path. What else did you want to do that you didn't?"

"Besides be a professional cook? All kinds of things. A writer. A party planner. A florist. I had changed my mind a hundred times growing up, but I always came back to the joy of cooking. Cooking is how I dealt with all my marital problems. I'd try new recipes, then give them to my friends to eat."

"It's not too late."

She took a deep breath for courage. "For you either."

"What do you mean?"

"Take Bash's offer. Be the head chef in Jersey City."

"But then I have to leave town."

"I know. And I wish that weren't the case, but you will always regret it if you turn down this opportunity. I can see it every time you talk about it. You have to do this, Mav. You're ready. I just don't think you realize it."

"You don't want me to stay?" He sat up and held her gaze.

"It doesn't matter what I want. This is your dream."

"I'm not sure I am ready."

"You are. Trust me. Staying in Candlewood Falls isn't going to ease any of the guilt. You're always going to grieve for your wife just like I'm always going to grieve for my mom. But you're here amongst the living, and you have to keep moving forward. Jersey City is that direction."

"You're throwing me out." He cupped her face.

She placed her hand over his. "You were never going to stay for long. We have now and few days until the competition. Let's enjoy them."

"Are you going to go after your dreams too?"

"As soon as I figure them out." She kissed him then because she didn't want to talk anymore. She had too many questions swirling in her head about what her direction actually was. She only wanted to enjoy the moment.

The sun had dropped further, washing out the day's colors. Lying on the blanket, amongst the brown trunks of the apple trees, the shadows covered them, shielded them even. They kissed and touched with a tenderness they hadn't shared before. They took their time making love, exploring each other's bodies. She wanted him to know what she was feeling for him without having to say it. He was the kind of man dreams were made from. She had waited her whole life for a man like him to come along. She didn't know that she wouldn't be able to keep him. That wasn't the story she had written in her head.

She wanted him to live his dream because he deserved to be happy. And she wanted him to know that she had fallen in love with him like no other man before him. But that she understood he wasn't hers to keep.

With every touch and stroke, he seemed to be saying the same to her. When there was nothing between them except the heat of their skin, he entered her slowly, deliberately, filling her up with everything she needed. They rocked together until the end, neither saying a word, but keeping their gazes locked. She didn't want to miss a second of him. Afterward, they lay wrapped in each other's trembling arms, a tear running down each of their faces.

CHAPTER TWENTY-FIVE

Petra stood in the damp grass. The wet blades sticking between her toes. Her cup of coffee grew cold as she evaluated the cloud coverage from her backyard. The thick haze was low and ominous, the promise of something ugly in their future. She would give anything for a few cheery white cottony puffs bouncing around in a bright-blue sky.

The morning had barely stretched out and the humidity was as thick as Challah bread. Nothing would ease the oppressive heat except a really strong thunderstorm. She would welcome the relief, but not the storm. And one was predicted this afternoon. Gusts of twenty miles an hour. Torrential rain. All during the competition. Her hands shook against the porcelain of the mug.

She had to try and rise above her fears. They stood to lose a lot if she allowed her fear of storms to get in her way. Somewhere inside her was bravery. All she had to do was dig it out. As long as Mav was with her through it all, she would be able to keep her head on straight. She was safe with him. After today, she would find a way to battle her fears without him.

She had been doing a lot of thinking amongst all the practicing for today and the time she and Mav had carved out for themselves. Those moments had been few, but she cherished every one of them. Her life would change this time. She didn't want to be the woman waking up every morning with regret.

"Mom, what are you doing out here? Don't you have to get ready?" Paige stood beside her. Her hair was still wet from a shower. She wore a Wilde Orchard t-shirt tied at her hip. Her shorts defied gravity.

"I have a few hours." She turned back to the sky. Would it be too much to ask for a delay in the storm? She said a silent prayer to her mother for a little help today.

"I was thinking that maybe after work today I could tackle that corner in the basement. The one with all Christmas decorations," Paige said, bringing her back to the humid morning.

"Really?" Paige hadn't wanted much to do with the packing. She hadn't blamed her. The job was for the birds. But she had learned something valuable about her mother because of it. That was a blessing. She was going to learn to find those in the dark clouds too.

"I didn't get to say goodbye. Maybe this will help with that. I don't know. I just want to help." Paige pulled on the edge of her shirt.

"I think that's great." She took a risk and put a hand on Paige's face. Paige gifted her a smile. Boy, things were changing. "I was thinking about something too. Your dad should be in his new place by now. I haven't talked to him, but that was the plan. You could live there with him, if you want. And you don't have to go to school." That had been something she had been up with a lot lately. Paige deserved to have her dreams come true too.

"Are you serious?"

"Sure. Your dad would like you to live there."

"Not about Dad. I don't want to live with him. I mean about school. You're going to stop pushing me?"

"School is my dream. Not yours. At least not now. If you change your mind, someday, then it will be because of you." It took her mother's note, the photo album, and the unfinished cookbook to get her to see that she and Paige needed to live their lives their way.

"Thanks, Mom. I want to stay in Candlewood Falls and work at the orchard."

"Why would you want to do that? This isn't a town for a young person. It's the place people come to raise their children."

"I like it here."

"Don't stay because of Junior. There are a million Juniors out there and if he is the special one, he'll wait."

"It's not because of him. It's because you're here."

"Me?"

"I want to stay with you. If that's okay."

"It's more than okay. It's perfect." She folded Paige into a hug and held her tightly. She didn't know when another hug was coming. This one would have to last.

"Great. After work, I'll stop by the competition to see how you're doing. And then I'll start on the basement."

"Hopefully the weather holds."

"Don't worry. You're going to be great." Paige trotted back inside the house.

Miracles never ceased.

Mav checked the trunk. He had everything they would need today, all the ingredients and cooking utensils not supplied by the competition. He even packed things they may not need at all, but he didn't want them going without. And if someone had a great idea at the last second, or there was a twist to a challenge—very likely—they would be ready.

He had driven to his storage unit where he had put away all his supplies from his old life. He hadn't been inside in three years. At first the stale smell and the sight of so many pots, pans, and knives choked him. He had a hundred cookbooks. Awards he had won had been stacked in boxes along with a ton of photos of him with other celebrity chefs. He scoured through everything as if it all had belonged to someone else. And it had.

He would try to be behind the scenes this time with his new restaurant. He wanted to remain anonymous in the kitchen, but Bash had said that wasn't possible. His name was the selling feature. His name would pack the seats and without that, the place would fail. Bash never failed. He wished he had his brother's luck.

The weather was failing them today. The forecast called for storms during the competition time. They couldn't lose Petra to her fears. She had to run the show. He couldn't give one instruction.

His phone rang deep in his pocket. Bash's name popped up on the screen. "What's up?"

"I need you to come to the restaurant."

"Sure. When?" He slid into the driver's seat.

"Today."

A laugh burst from his lips. Bash was silent on the other end. "You're not joking."

"I'm sorry, man. We're ordering all the kitchen appliances and gadgets and stuff. I don't know the first thing about that. You need to tell us what you want."

"I can't come today. That will have to wait until tomorrow." He kicked over the engine and turned around in the storage facility parking lot.

"Can't do it. I'm on a plane tonight and going to Houston for two weeks. And the big boss, Rick, needs to know how much we're spending... like yesterday. He's got someone coming in to redo the floors and all the tables and chairs. He's freaking over the money."

"But the space is perfect. I thought we weren't changing a thing." He pulled into traffic.

"Rick changed his mind. Has a new vision."

"Then why didn't we take the Candlewood Falls place?" If he had known that Rick was ready to renovate, he would've pushed harder to stay in town. He didn't want to relocate again. He didn't want to live in Jersey City no matter how nice the waterfront area was now.

The sky took on an ominous turn as if it too was annoyed with the new revelation. For spite now, the sky would betray him and open its anger up on the competition.

"Because Jersey City has a hell of a lot more people in it. The tomatoes are just as good on that side of the Garden State as they are in town. What time can you be here?"

"Bash, I have the competition today. We're down a student. I have to step in." Not to mention, he wanted to be there for Petra if and when the storm showed up. He hit the turn signal at the traffic light and made a right on red.

"Delegate. That's what a good chef does, right? You said yourself, you didn't want to hog the spotlight this time. Start with this class. Let your lady take the lead. She can't need you that badly."

She didn't need him at all. In fact, he had assumed she was worried about the storm today, but she hadn't said a word to him all day. Maybe she had a plan in the works to deal with her anxiety. A plan that didn't include him. Even the way she had been making love with him said she was preparing for their inevitable end. She had made up her mind that he wasn't going to be a part of this new version of herself. And he couldn't change it. Why did Bash have to pick now to spotlight the places he and Petra weren't working? Not that Bash knew he had done that.

"I have to drop off the supplies to them first. I'll be there in two hours." The first rain drop splattered on the windshield, blurring his view.

"Make it ninety minutes. And don't be late." Bash ended the call.

CHAPTER TWENTY-SIX

"What do you mean you can't stay?" Petra searched Mav's face for some attempt at a bad joke, but all she found was the downturn of his lips and a painful expression pooling in his eyes.

"I'm sorry. I have to go pick out the kitchen appliances and cookware. Today's the only day it can be done."

"But why? Can't you order that stuff online?"

"Not the appliances. Everything has to be measured. I need to see it."

"What about us? How can you leave us?" The wind had picked up, whipping her hair in her face. A few fat raindrops hit her in the head. They were in the parking lot outside the Candlewood Falls Country Club—the competition spot.

The banquet hall's windows looked down on them and onto the golf course speckled with trees already losing leaves to the wind. The competition would be inside that room with a full view of the storm.

The judges had arrived before even she got there. All

the other competitors were unpacking their supplies and hurrying them inside before the skies really let loose. They were behind schedule because of Mav's little announcement and now they would surely lose without him.

"You and Niko will be fine."

"We're down an extra pair of hands. Can't you go after the competition?" Somewhere in the distance, the rumble of thunder like a bass drum pounded in her belly. "Did you hear that?"

"Hear what?"

"The thunder, Mav. Didn't you hear it?" She was pretty sure the rumble happened again, but she could be imagining it.

"I don't hear anything. Petra, please try and understand." He shook his head.

"I don't understand. I can't believe you would ditch us now."

"Ask Ember to step in for me, if it's only the pair of hands you need."

"You know what I mean." Of course, she needed more than his hands. He had to be her rock when that lightning started going off.

"You don't need me. But I need this new job." He popped open his trunk. "Everything for today is in here. I'll help you bring in the boxes. Then I have to go."

She pulled out the first box and plopped it on the ground. "Don't bother. Niko and I will bring in everything. Like you said, we don't need you."

Before she ran inside and grabbed Niko, she sent a text to Ember asking her to come and help. The thunder replied instead. She wanted to shout to the sky that she wasn't afraid. That the storm couldn't beat her, but her lips clamped down over every word.

Every time Mav tried to reach for a box, she shoved him away.

"For God's sake, Petra, let the man help. We're wasting time." Niko glared at her.

"Fine. But for Niko."

The last box was stored by their competition station. The room was a cacophony of voices and metal clanking against glass as the competitors prepared their places. Mav shifted from one foot to the other.

"That's it. You know what to do. You've practiced this. You two are going to be great," he said.

Niko stuck out his hand. "Thanks. For everything. I've enjoyed your class. I promise to come out to your new restaurant."

"Thanks, Niko. I've really liked teaching you."

She bit back a cackle. *He liked teaching*, her backside. She tied the apron around her waist.

Mav leaned in by her ear. "Don't be worried about the storm."

She held his gaze and recalled that great saying about the warrior being the storm. "Whatever."

When he turned to go, she wanted to run after him and tell him it was okay. That she understood what he had to do. That in a few days they would all forget about this silly competition and get on with their lives without each other. She wanted to tell him all his dreams would come true and he deserved each and every one of them. She wanted to tell him the storm scared the hell out of her and she needed him right beside her or she wouldn't be able to cook one damn thing.

Instead, she turned to Niko. "Looks like it's just you and me."

Petra paced in the ladies' room with its fancy hand towels and marble sinks. The storm raged outside, shaking this building like the big bad wolf. Her hands dripped sweat. She repeatedly wiped them on her pants, but the sweat came right back. Her stomach was filled with battery acid style bile. Her mind jumped through a hundred different thoughts. She could not cook.

Right after she had made her *you and me* declaration to Niko, the lightning had lit up the sky, and she had run for cover. *Coward.* She splashed cold water on her face.

"Petra, are you in here?" Ember peeked around the mahogany bathroom door.

"I'll be right out."

Ember handed her a paper towel. It was soft and smelled like vanilla. "If you don't look out the window, you don't even know the storm is going on."

"Ha. The whole building is ready to come off its foundation."

"You can do this."

"I can't. Not without Mav." She should not have sent him away. But he had been ready to go. She couldn't make him stay.

"He's not here, sis. You're in charge. If you don't get out there right now, the judges are going to disqualify your team."

She couldn't allow that to happen. "Why couldn't I be afraid of heights instead?"

"What fun would that be?" Ember grabbed her by the elbow. "Come on. We have food to make."

One side of the room was nothing but floor-to-ceiling windows, beautiful for a bride and groom to dance in front of, but torturous for her. The scene outside the windows was frightening. The trees were bent in half. The rain pounded on the windows to be let in. The lights flickered overhead. She swallowed the knot in her throat.

"You're not alone," Ember whispered in her ear. "We're all here for you. See?"

Standing at the station set up for her and Niko was also Titi in her bright makeup and colorful clothes. Her smile broke open.

"Hello, sweetie. Niko called in an SOS. I'm here to help." Titi pulled her into a gardenia-infused hug.

Tears stung her eyes. "Thank you."

"I'll be right over here if you need me," Ember said. "With your cheering section." Sitting in the audience was Raf and Brad and Brad's girlfriend, Lyra. Paige sat with Junior who waved.

Her phone buzzed in her pocket. She grabbed it, hoping it was Mav. Instead, a text came through from her sister Nyx. *Kick ass, big sis.* Tears stung her eyes again and not from all of Titi's perfume.

She could be brave, even with the storm raging outside, because she wasn't alone. For all the things she had done wrong in her life, all the dreams she had left on the table, she was still loved. And that was what mattered most.

She grabbed Niko's and Titi's hands. On a heavy sigh, she said, "Looks like it's showtime."

Mav turned up his windshield wipers, and he still couldn't see. The roads were flooding. Nothing but a line of red taillights was in front of him. He wasn't going anywhere in this storm, and it was stupid to try. He'd probably end up dead.

His breath stuck in his throat. How could he even think such a thing when his wife had died in a storm much like this one? What had Shelby been thinking in her last moments? He always hoped they hadn't been hateful thoughts of him. Why hadn't she turned around or gotten off the road sooner? He had asked that question a million times with no way to have an answer. All he had were regrets.

He hit the brakes. The car in front of him had come to a sudden stop. A wave of water sprayed over the car, making it impossible to see, but his vision was clear. He had to get off the highway and not just because of the weather, though that should be enough of a reason. He didn't want to live with any more regrets. Every mile he drove away from Candlewood Falls and Petra, the remorse piled up. He belonged with her, and he would do whatever it took to make her see that. So what if she didn't need him? She wanted him. That much was evident. She had said it in every way possible including getting mad at him for leaving her today. He had walked away from love before for work. He wouldn't do it twice.

He also had a competition to get to. He put on his turn signal and crawled across three rows of traffic until he was in the exit lane.

The contest had already started, but if he took backroads, he might make it for the dessert round. No team was being eliminated. This contest was for points. The team with the most points at the end won. At least his two students won't be out of the game before he could make things right.

He voice-activated his phone and called Bash.

"Where are you?" Bash's voice filled the car.

"I'm not coming."

"What are you talking about? Is it the weather? It's not that bad here."

"I don't care if the sun is shining where you are. I'm not coming. In fact, I'm not going to take the job unless we put the restaurant in Candlewood Falls. Tell Rick not to bother with his renos. I'm not interested in another high-end city food establishment. I want a small restaurant where all the patrons know each other."

He turned on his high beams and increased the speed of his wipers, hoping he made it back in time and that Petra would forgive him.

"You've lost your mind, Mav. We can't back out now. The lease has been signed. Permits have been requested. Get your ass here now and pick out your stove before I find you and choke the life out of you."

"I'm sorry, Sebastian. I really am. I would never do anything to hurt you. But I can't take you up on your offer. You'll have to find another name to be the star of your show." The rain made traveling difficult still. He had no idea if he was even on the right side of the road.

"Sebastian, huh? Well, you must be serious then. You're making a big mistake, Maverick. You won't bounce back from this. You'll be forced to keep teaching at the college to a bunch of students who don't give a damn about cooking the way you used to."

"Maybe. All I know is right now, I need to get to my students. They need me, and I let them down. If I'm ever going to lead a team again, it would do me good to remember how to be a good leader. And that's get in the trenches with my team."

"You would be a good leader here in Jersey City."

"It's not for me. Thank you for trying to get me off my ass. I needed it. But what I want doesn't have a view of the New York City skyline." He wanted the view of the beautiful woman in his kitchen, working her lip under her teeth while she wound her way through a recipe. Or the view of that same beautiful woman lying naked in his bed, calling out his name because he made her feel things no one else had.

Hopefully, he wasn't too late.

CHAPTER TWENTY-SEVEN

Sweat burned Petra's eyes. The heat and smoke from the grill were in her hair and in her pores. She would smell liked grilled pork for weeks. She was sure of it.

The contest wasn't going well. The storm continued to distract her. Every time the lightning lit up the windows to the side of her, her focus jumped. The sausage was overcooked. Titi wilted the onions and peppers again. Niko had dropped the beans on the floor. They hadn't had time to make a new batch. They had to fall back on a salad.

"Attention, contestants," the judge with the platinum hair called out. She had on more makeup than a clown, and she wore a pink sheath dress with a ridiculous orchid pinned to the collar that was losing its petals all afternoon. One had fallen in their pasta salad. Niko had yanked it out before anyone else had noticed. "Challenge time. This is the dessert round and the final challenge of the day. In your dessert, you must include barbeque potato chips." Orchid lady held up a bag of Lays Potato Chips.

She bit back a groan. They were planning to make a key lime no bake pie. And they had been doing barbeque food all day. She really wanted another flavor. Wasabi balls would've been better at this point.

"What do we do?" Titi said, looking over her shoulder at the other contestants and back at her and Niko.

"No idea," Niko said. "Creativity isn't my thing. That's Mav's area."

"Yeah, well, he isn't here." She wished he was. She glanced over at Ember to see if an idea would channel between them, but she came up empty. Ember did give her a thumbs-up, though.

They didn't have a chance to win anyway. They had lost the other two rounds. Even if they pulled off the best dessert in Jersey, they wouldn't have enough points. Thunder and lightning roared at the same time. She jumped. They might as well back out now and save face. Anything she could come up with that included barbeque-flavored potato chips would suck.

"Petra, you need to find us an idea," Titi said. "The other teams have already started working."

And the clock was ticking.

"Guys, I have no clue. I think we're washed up here. Let's cut our losses."

"You want to quit?" Niko said. "Now?"

She looked between Niko and Titi. She stole a glance back out to the audience. Paige watched with anticipation on her face. Was she really going to quit in front of her daughter? Hadn't she just told her daughter to go for her dreams?

Well, what were her dreams? Did she want to win this thing? She did. But it wasn't just winning the contest. She wanted to finish what her mother started. She wanted to turn those pages into a real cookbook for her mother. And then she wanted to make those very recipes in her own place. A small café with her name above the door. A place where her friends and family could come and sit for hours, laugh, share, be safe. And brave.

The thunder shook the building again. A loud gasp came from the audience area. She took a deep breath. She was safe. She was okay. She was loved. And dammit, she was the storm.

"Okay, how about a dip to go with the chips?"

"You can do better than that." The deep voice was right behind her. The shivers that ran over her skin had nothing to do with the storm outside.

She turned and flew into Mav's arms. He scooped her up and swung her around. His clothes were wet from the rain. But he was strong and solid. And he was here.

Niko high-fived him. Titi did a happy dance with her dish towel. The other teams turned to see what all the fuss was about. One guy's face dropped. *Yup, buddy.*

"What are you doing here?" she said.

"I'm sorry to all of you. I never should've left you alone today. That's the worst thing a teacher and a head chef could ever do. I hope you'll forgive me."

"Forgiven," Niko said. "Enough yapping. We need a dessert idea. We've wasted a lot of time."

"I can't tell you what to do. You have to come up with the idea on your own. But I can give a hint. Think what you would want on a hot summer day after a barbeque. Stick with our theme. All American." Mav leaned in while he spoke, keeping his voice down, but encouraging them with every syllable.

"Ice cream," she said, picturing the finished product all at once. They could use waffle cones and dip the ends in chocolate too.

"Exactly," Mav said.

"But we don't have time for that," Niko said.

"I brought a machine that allows you to make no churn ice cream. Niko, it's in that big red bin."

Niko ran.

"What else?" Mav said.

"How about if we mix in some of the typical flavors in ice cream as a base?" Titi said.

"Now we're thinking like a team." Mav clapped his hands. Titi's smile was triumphant.

They rushed around their station, mixing, turning, and preparing. Mav scooped the ice cream into the cones and placed them upside down on the plate. Titi added more chips as a garnish on the side. The final product was beautiful.

They waited, holding their breaths while the judges tried all the contestants' desserts.

"And the winner is…"

CHAPTER TWENTY-EIGHT

The storm blew east, leaving patches of a pink and orange sky as the sun took a final farewell over the rolling hills. The air had cooled enough, Petra needed a light sweater.

She and Mav put the last of the boxes into his trunk. He pushed it closed and leaned against the car. She fit herself between his long legs and wrapped her arms around his neck. She must smell like sweat and grilled food and who knew what else. She should probably insist on a shower before forcing him to be so close to her, but she couldn't think of one single place she'd rather be than in his arms.

"I'm sorry you didn't win." His hands held her waist.

"Looks like we're all failing class."

"Yeah, about that. I already handed in your grades. You all got As."

"Seriously?"

"Yup. Even Titi."

"Is that why she showed up today?"

"You'll have to ask her. I had nothing to do with it. But I'm glad she was here to help you both when I wasn't. I never should've left you."

"You needed to. You have a dream waiting for you. But I was glad you came back. Everything had gone wrong all day. I just wanted us to win one round."

"You won dessert."

"Thanks to you."

"Wrong. Thanks to you. You came up with the ice cream idea."

"But you had the machine."

He shrugged. "Anyone would've thought to bring it."

"Are you going to Jersey City now?"

"About that. I turned down the offer."

"Why did you do that? It's your dream to have a restaurant again."

"I realized as I was driving in that awful storm that my dream means nothing without you in it. How would you feel about me sticking around town for a while?"

"You're going to teach?"

"No, not that. I'm thinking I might try a small farm-to-table idea right here in town. Buy that space by the mill. See what happens. What do you think?"

"I think that's a fantastic idea."

"And what about you?"

"I want to put my mother's recipes in a book. And maybe open a small place of my own. Nothing big. Breakfast and lunch maybe."

"Well, if you're interested, I hear there's a washed-up chef looking to hire. He's a real pain to work for, but the perks are good."

"What perks would that be?" She snuggled against him.

"He makes breakfast in bed. Clothing optional." He kissed her neck under her ear, making her squirm with delight.

"I don't have a lot of experience."

"On the job training." His lips made a trail to her collarbone.

"Is clothing optional there too?"

"As long as it's in his private kitchen. He doesn't like to share the help."

"Hard to argue with that. I love you, Mav."

"And I love you."

EPILOGUE

One month later.

O Petra never touched an alpaca before. All the years the Sunny Side Up Farm was in her backyard practically, but she never stepped foot on it until today. Today was a celebration. A celebration for Ruby and a celebration for the future in so many ways. And for Petra, a celebration for being brave.

"They don't bite," her cousin Brooklyn said, laughing. Brooklyn glowed with the sun on her face and one hand absently rubbing her belly. "This one is Alpacino. He's everyone's favorite. And that one is Alistair. He's a hero around here."

Petra shook out some of the alpaca food Brooklyn gave her in a bag and let this Alpacino creature eat out of her hand. "It tickles," she said.

"They make the best pets. You have to come by more often and spend time with them."

"I would love that."

"And me too. Please spend time with me too now that

you're sticking around Candlewood Falls. I think we should start a Wilde girls' getaway."

"That sounds great. Maybe in a few months?" She glanced at Brooklyn's belly pushing against her white top.

"Caleb would appreciate that."

"Yes, I would, please. And after the wedding. Otherwise, this woman will never marry me." Caleb pulled Brooklyn into his arms and kissed her on the cheek.

"I guess I never do anything the way I'm supposed to." Brooklyn smiled up at Caleb.

"Neither do I," Ember said, holding Raf's hand in the air. Raf just shook his head, but his smile said it all. He loved her sister. And for that, Petra was grateful.

Petra searched the crowd for Mav. Her other cousins were at the farm too. Brad and Lyra sat under the big oak tree, deep in conversation. Brad wrapped one of those muscular arms of his around Lyra and pulled her close. She rested her head on his shoulder. Brad's daughter, Winter, hurried over to Brad to show him something. Petra couldn't make it out from where she stood, but Brad's face beamed. He high-fived his girl, and she brushed his long hair away from his face.

Her other cousins, Sam and Lacey, sat at the picnic table with their significant others. Sam was still in his suit from the memorial service they had held for Ruby earlier today. The four of them were having their cards read by Sam's girlfriend, Faith.

Her father sat in a patio chair next to his brother Silas. They were talking about something she couldn't hear. But Huck waved away whatever Silas had said. That had Silas throwing back his head and roaring in that deep Wilde timbre all the men had. Huck busted out laughing too. It was good to see her father happy for the moment. Paige made him happy too which was why she and Paige would be staying with him for the time being.

Her gaze finally rested on Mav. He smiled at her, and she was lost in him. The rest of the farm drifted away. He came to her and pulled her into his arms.

"Hey there," he said. "You doing okay?"

"I'm doing great. This was a perfect way to honor my mom. I just wish Nyx could've been here."

"You and your sisters will just have to do something else when she comes out for the holidays."

"I hope so."

"Your family is great. There's so much love here." Mav's gaze turned to her loved ones.

"I don't know why I stayed away for so long." At one time, distance seemed like her only answer, but that had been fear talking. Now she was in charge and staying in the place that was in her heart.

"You're back now. And you're not going anywhere." He placed a soft kiss on her lips.

"Thanks to you."

"You had more to do with staying than I did. In fact, I was running for the hills when you had your feet firmly planted."

"Take some credit, Mav. You made all my dreams come true. No one has ever done that for me."

"If you'll let me, I'd like to make every new dream come true too. Just so you'll smile up at me the way you are right now."

"Sounds like the offer of a lifetime."

He placed another kiss on her lips. "Oh, the offer is definitely for a lifetime."

ALSO BY STACEY WILK

Serenity Series
Sea Glass Made with Second Chances
Sea Glass Hidden in Plain Sight
Sea Glass Out of Balance
Sea Glass Wrapped in Red
Heritage River Series
The Risk for House and Home
The Bridge Between Love and Lies
The Essence of Whiskey and Tea
Hometown Series
Taking Root
Raising Winter
Defining Chances
Beginning Over
Steeling Hearts
Whispering Christmas
Winter at the Shore Series
No More Darkness
Through the Darkness

Light Upon the Darkness

The Brotherhood Protectors World
Winter's Last Chance
The Last Betrayal
Her Last Word
The Last Days of Christmas
Seduced by Denial
Chill in the Air
Fighting for Tessa
Nash's Promise
Cruz's Watch
Harlan Unleashed
<u>Big Sky Country Series</u>
Time Won't Erase
Stay Awhile
Love Never Ends
Dare to Tell (coming soon)

ACKNOWLEDGMENTS

~

Because I'm a small business, I do much of the heavy lifting myself which makes my thank you page a little light.

However, I have to always thank Jen and Kathy for taking this journey with me and creating our beloved town Candlewood Falls. I hope we'll be able to create more stories here in the future.

I have to thank the incomparable Robin Rottner. She finds the missing pieces in the stories so I can glue them back together.

I also want to thank my Facebook reader group for choosing the name Paige for Petra's daughter. For any reader that didn't like that mother and daughter's names both started with P, please forgive me. When my reader group speaks up, I listen.

ABOUT THE AUTHOR

From an early age, best selling author Stacey Wilk told tales as a way to escape. At six she wrote short stories in composition notebooks, at twelve she wrote a novel on a typewriter, in high school biology she wrote rock star romances in her binder instead of paying attention.

But it wasn't until many years later, inspired by her children and a looming birthday, that she finally took her story-telling seriously. And published her first novel in 2013. Since then, she's gone on to publish thirty-one more so women everywhere could fall in love and find an escape of their own.

She isn't done telling stories. Not by a long shot. If you want to read her best selling, emotional, and honest books about family, romance, and second chances, visit her at www.staceywilk.com

∾